A Fur-out Haircut!

"*Dad!* You gotta talk to Erin, and then I'm gonna *kill* her!"

"That sounds a little drastic." Doc bent down to give Teddy a hug and a kiss. "What's the problem?"

"Jocko, that's what!" Teddy said. "He's *bald*!"

"Oh, Teddy, he is not." Erin came out of the living room and stood on tiptoe to kiss Doc on the cheek. "Hi, Daddy. Hi, Vallie. You're awfully late — Teddy and I already ate, but there's plenty left."

"He is too bald!" Teddy scowled at her from under the visor of the Phillies baseball cap he always wore. "He doesn't have any fur on his rear end!"

D0981568

ANIMAL INN

THE PET MAKEOVER

Virginia Vail

AN
APPLE
PAPERBACK

SCHOLASTIC INC.
New York Toronto London Auckland Sydney

No part of this publication may be reproduced in whole or in part, or stored in a retrieval system, or transmitted in any form or by any means, electronic, mechanical, photocopying, recording, or otherwise, without written permission of the publisher. For information regarding permission, write to Scholastic Inc., 730 Broadway, New York, NY 10003.

ISBN 0-590-42798-9

Copyright © 1990 by Cloverdale Press and Jane Thornton. All rights reserved. Published by Scholastic Inc. APPLE PAPERBACKS is a registered trademark of Scholastic Inc.

12 11 10 9 8 7 6 5 4 3 2 1   0 1 2 3 4 5/9

Printed in the U.S.A.   11

First Scholastic printing, March 1990

For Meg, Jennifer, Nick, Deborah, Jamie, Kim, Mary, Stacy, Jeff, Michelle, and all the other fans of **Animal Inn** who have written such wonderful letters to me.

Chapter
1

"Dad, they're going to be all right, aren't they?" Valentine Taylor asked anxiously. She was sitting in the fresh, sweet-smelling straw that covered the floor of the birthing stall, the exhausted heifer's head in her lap. As she spoke, she stroked Lulu gently.

"Yes, Vallie, both Lulu and her calf are going to be just fine," her father, Dr. Theodore Taylor, assured her. He stood up, stripped off his rubber gloves, and wiped his perspiring face on his shirt sleeve. Looking at Toby Curran, who was hanging over the stall door with a worried look on his face, Doc grinned. "Congratulations, Toby. You have a fine calf there. I wouldn't be surprised if she turned out to be a 4-H prize winner just like her mother."

"If she's okay, why is she just lying there?" Toby asked. "And why did it take so long for her to be born?"

"She's lying there *because* it took her so long to be born," Doc said. "She was determined to come into the world backwards, and I had to turn her around so she could make a proper entrance, head and forefeet first. It's a good thing your dad called me when he did, or she might not have made it."

"Look, Dad!" Val cried. "Lulu's standing up!"

The heifer struggled to her feet and immediately began licking the newborn. As Val, Doc, and Toby watched, the little calf quivered all over and raised its head. A few minutes later it too managed to stand up, wobbling groggily.

"Hooray!" Toby cheered. "She *is* okay!"

"Of course she is," Val said, as proud as if she had delivered the calf herself. She smiled as the calf tottered to Lulu's side and began to nurse. No matter how many times she saw her father bring a new animal into the world, each birth was a special thrill. That was one of the reasons Val wanted to be a veterinarian like Doc, and why she loved working at Animal Inn after school and on Saturdays. Toby worked there, too. He was fourteen, only one year older than Val, and one of her very best friends. "What are you going to call her, Toby?"

"She ought to have a special name — she's a real beauty," Doc said.

"She's a beauty, all right," Toby agreed. "Hey, that's it! That's what I'll call her. Beauty!" He reached out and shook Doc's hand vigorously. "Thanks, Doc.

I was real worried, since it's Lulu's first time, but I should've known you'd pull her through. You're the best vet in Essex, Pennsylvania!"

Doc laughed. "I'm also the *only* vet in Essex, Pennsylvania, Toby. But thanks for the kind words." He closed his medical bag, patted Lulu's bony rump, and let himself out of the stall. Lulu paid no attention. She just chewed her cud calmly, as though Beauty were her tenth calf instead of her first. She seemed to have forgotten already what a hard time she'd had. Val wondered why people couldn't be as casual about having babies as animals were.

"If I ever get married and have children," she said, "I hope my doctor's as good as you are, Dad. But if I'm going to be a vet, I probably won't have time to get married. I'll be too busy taking care of my patients."

Laughing, Doc put his arm around her shoulders and gave her a hug. "You won't have to worry about that for some time yet," he said. "But what we do have to worry about is getting home in time for supper. You know how Mrs. Racer scolds us when we're late."

Mrs. Racer was the Taylors' elderly housekeeper. She watched over their household like a broody hen and loved Doc, Val, and Val's younger brother and sister, eight-year-old Teddy and eleven-

3

year-old Erin, as though they were her own family. When Val's mother had died three years ago in an automobile accident, it was Mrs. Racer who had comforted them all and helped them through that terrible time. Val felt much closer to Mrs. Racer than to her own grandparents, whom she rarely saw because they lived so far away.

"See you tomorrow, Toby," Val said as she climbed into the dark blue Animal Inn van that was parked outside the Currans' dairy barn. "And say hi to your mom and dad for me."

"I will." Toby went around to the driver's side where Doc was buckling his seat belt. "I'll bring you Dad's check, too, Doc, so you won't have to send him a bill."

Doc shook his head. "No need, Toby. You're a friend of the family, and I don't charge my friends. Besides, you've been a big help to me at Animal Inn."

"Yeah, but you saved Beauty's life and Lulu's, too. I'm going to chip in some of my own money — I want to, because they're my animals," Toby insisted.

Val poked Doc gently in the ribs. "Don't argue," she said in a whisper. "Mr. Curran's one of our clients who always pays up, and he can afford it. And so can Toby."

Currans' Dairy Farm was successful and prosperous, and so were the several ice-cream parlors in the area that Mr. Curran owned and operated. Unlike many of Animal Inn's patrons, who had little money to spare, and who often paid Doc for his services in eggs, sausages, or produce from their farms, Mr. Curran never ran up a bill.

"We'll talk about it tomorrow," Doc said to Toby. Then he added with a grin, "Tell you what — suppose you tell your dad that I'll make a deal with him. All the ice cream the Taylor family can eat — free of charge — the next time we go to the ice-cream parlor, all right?"

"And considering how much ice cream Teddy can put away, it'll probably cost more than Dad's bill," Val teased.

"I guess he'd be willing to risk it," Toby said solemnly. "But only if I can come, too!" He laughed.

Doc started the engine. "Congratulations again."

Val leaned out the window and waved as the van moved away. She suddenly realized that her stomach was complaining loudly. The veggie burger she'd had for lunch at Hamilton Junior High was only a vague memory, and she was starving.

She wondered what Mrs. Racer had prepared for supper, hoping it was macaroni and cheese with tuna, one of her favorite casseroles. The rest of the family liked it, too, which meant that Mrs. Racer wouldn't have to fix two different main dishes as she often did — a meat dish for Doc, Erin, and Teddy, and a meatless one for Val. Val just couldn't bring herself to eat anything that had once been walking around on four legs (or, in the case of chickens, two legs). Mrs. Racer didn't seem to mind the extra work, but it sometimes made Val feel guilty.

"Did I just hear a rumble?" Doc asked, glancing over at her. "Or is there something wrong with the engine?"

"It's me, all right," Val admitted. "Am I hungry!"

"Me, too," Doc said. "It's been such a long day, I think I forgot to eat lunch. Things are more hectic than usual, with all the construction going on."

"Yes, I know. But it'll be over soon, and then it's going to be wonderful." Val sighed happily. "It'll be so great once Animal Inn has boarding kennels. Maybe there won't be so many abandoned pets when their owners know there's a place where they can board their cats and dogs when they go away for vacation. I took two reservations for the kennel this afternoon, and Pat said she had booked four before I came in." Pat Dempwolf was Doc's receptionist.

"I bet by the time we open in mid-June, we'll have a full house!"

"And don't forget the extra treatment room and our bigger infirmary," Doc reminded her. "I don't know where we'd put all our patients if the bank hadn't approved the loan to expand the clinic. Good thing your friend Mr. Merrill is an officer of the Essex Savings and Loan, Vallie. Otherwise we might have ended up housing some sick animals in the barn. How do you think The Ghost would like sharing his stall with a couple of sick puppies?"

"Oh, Dad, you'd have gotten the loan even if Mr. Merrill wasn't a big wheel at the bank. And he's not really my friend. For a while there, I thought he was my enemy, when he wanted you to destroy The Ghost." Val shuddered at the memory of how her beloved Gray Ghost, Mr. Merrill's beautiful dapple gray champion jumper, had almost lost his life because he couldn't see well enough to compete in horse shows anymore. If Val hadn't used every penny she'd saved to buy The Ghost from Mr. Merrill and his snobby daughter, Cassandra, he'd have been put down. But now The Ghost was her own horse, and she loved him almost as much as she loved her family.

"Well, Mr. Merrill thinks you're pretty special,"

Doc said, glancing over at her and smiling warmly. "Which just proves that he knows a good thing when he sees it. I think we ought to invite him to our party to celebrate the opening of the boarding kennel, don't you?"

After a moment's hesitation, Val said, "I guess so. Does that mean Cassandra will come, too? And if she does, do I have to be nice to her?"

Doc laughed. "A little nice — not a lot. Anyway, I doubt if she'll be in town. The last time I spoke to Mr. Merrill, he said she was going to Europe as soon as her school lets out at the end of May."

"Good!" Val said. "In that case, I think we should invite the Merrills, along with all the other people who bring their pets to Animal Inn. We ought to invite the pets, too — they deserve a party. I bet most of them have never gone to a party in their whole lives! And if we're going to have lots of good food for the people, then we ought to have special treats for the animals, too. Toby and I could plan a menu for the dogs and cats and guinea pigs and gerbils and rabbits and hamsters — "

"Whoa!" Doc said. "Next you'll be suggesting that we should entertain every farm animal I've ever treated, including the sheep, cows, and goats. I'll have to take out another loan just to feed all our four-footed guests!"

Val giggled. "Well, maybe not the cows. They're awfully big, and they'd take up a lot of space. But hay doesn't cost much, and neither does stuff like carrots and apples. And we have lots of kibble and pellets for the other animals. I want this to be a really super party!"

Doc steered the van onto Old Mill Road, slowing down as they approached the Taylors' big old stone house. "I guess maybe tonight after supper you, Teddy, Erin, and I ought to sit down and start making some plans for this celebration. If the workers finish on schedule, our grand opening is only four weeks away."

"Oh, yes — let's," Val said eagerly. "Mrs. Racer's already promised to bake cookies and brownies, and Erin said she'd help her. My friend Jill wants to help out, too, and she's very good at organizing things. Could she come over tonight for our meeting?"

"Okay," Doc agreed. "As I recall, Jill's also a terrific popcorn maker, and both animals and people like popcorn."

He drove the van into the driveway, and Val hopped out. "I'll call her right away."

She cut across the lawn and ran into the house. "Hi, everybody! We're home," she called. "Sorry we're late, but Toby's heifer just had her first calf!"

Val braced herself as Jocko, their shaggy little

9

black-and-white mongrel, and Sunshine, their big golden retriever, dashed into the hall barking happily and leaping up to welcome her home.

"Hey, guys, take it easy!" she cried, patting both furry heads and staggering backward as Sunshine planted his paws on her chest. "I haven't been gone that long!"

"Was it a boy or a girl?" Erin asked, coming out of the living room. As usual, she was wearing a leotard and tights, and her blonde hair was neatly arranged in a tight knot on the top of her head. Erin wanted to be a ballerina, like her mother, who had been with the Pennsylvania Ballet before she married Doc. Like her, Eric was slender and petite, while Val looked more like Doc — tall and rangy, with thick chestnut-brown hair.

"Girl," Val told her. "Toby named her Beauty, because that's what she is."

Erin shivered delicately. "Did you watch the whole thing? *Yuck!* It must have been messy."

"It wasn't messy at all," Val said cheerfully. "It was really neat! Where's Teddy?"

"He went over to Billy's after school," Erin said. "He ought to be home any minute. Hi, Daddy!"

She ran to throw her arms around Doc, who had just come in.

"Hi, honey. Is Mrs. Racer still here?" Doc asked.

"I sure am!" Mrs. Racer came out of the kitchen, wiping her hands on her apron. She was a Mennonite, one of the "Plain People." All her dresses were exactly the same except for the color. She wore a little white lawn cap perched on the back of her head over her silver hair.

"There's a tuna-macaroni casserole in the oven and the string beans are all ready," she said. "Erin made a lovely salad, and it's in the icebox, along with the dressing. M'son Henry'll be here any minute now to pick me up. How's Toby's calf?"

"She couldn't be better," Doc said. "Toby's proud as punch."

"Glad to hear it." Mrs. Racer took off her apron and folded it neatly, handing it to Val. "Now don't forget, Vallie, that I'm not going to be here tomorrow — m'son Henry and me are going to my great-niece's wedding over in Star View. So you and Erin are going to have to do the shopping. I made out a list — I stuck it up with one of those magnet things on the icebox. Don't forget the bacon from Herman Stolzfus — that's the kind Doc likes. And Matthew Geist has the very best apples, so don't you dare buy 'em from anybody else. Erin knows where to go."

A car horn sounded, and Mrs. Racer hurried past

Val and Doc to the front door. "That's m'son Henry. See you Monday morning."

She bustled out and almost ran into Teddy, who was running in.

"Hi, Mrs. Racer. 'Bye, Mrs. Racer!" Teddy tossed his Phillies baseball cap on the table in the hall and ran to hug his dad. "What's for dinner?" he asked.

"Macaroni and tuna casserole," Mrs. Racer called over her shoulder. "And mind you help your sisters with the dishes!"

As the door closed behind her, Teddy said, "Hey, Dad, Sparky wants to help us with the party for the opening of the boarding thing, and I told her she could, all right? And I told her her cat could come, too. It's okay if Charlie comes, isn't it? He won't eat much."

"Of course Sparky can help," Doc said. "And Charlie is welcome, too. Go wash up, Teddy. Time for supper."

"Okay. But can Sparky eat over tonight? She doesn't eat much either."

"Tonight?" Erin said, taking the apron from Val and tying it around her waist.

"I don't see why not," Doc said. "If it's all right with Sparky's mother. Why don't you call her now?"

Val had already picked up the phone. "As soon as I call Jill."

"Oh, I don't need to call," Teddy said. He trotted into the kitchen and yelled out the back window, "Hey, Sparky, Dad says it's okay!" Then he ran back into the hall. "She was waiting in the backyard. She's already asked her mom."

"Good thing Mrs. Racer made an extra-big casserole," Erin muttered, as she set another place at the table.

Chapter
2

"Boy, that was good!" Philomena Sparks, commonly known as Sparky, said as she picked the last brownie crumb from her dessert plate and beamed. "The tuna casserole was almost as good as the ones my mom makes, and the brownies were great." She looked hopefully at the big cookie tin on the kitchen counter. "I don't s'pose there's any more brownies in there," she added hopefully.

"Yes, there are, but you can't have any more," Teddy said. "You ate two already, piggy!" He reached over and tugged one of Sparky's braids.

"I am *not* a piggy!"

"Yes, you are. You have pigtails — that proves it!"

"Teddy!" Doc warned. "Where are your manners? Sparky's our guest, remember."

Teddy rolled his eyes. "Oh, c'mon." Then he glanced mischievously at Sparky, saying in a sickly-sweet voice, "Would you like another brownie, Phil-o-meena?"

With an outraged squawk, Sparky lunged for him. "Don't you *dare* call me that, Teddy Taylor, or I'll break your face!"

"Ooo, I'm so scared! Help, help!" Teddy squealed, leaping out of his chair and dashing for the kitchen door. Sparky ran after him, laughing, followed by Jocko and Sunshine.

Erin sighed. "Honestly, those two!"

"They're something else, all right," Val said with a grin. "More coffee, Dad?"

"No thanks, honey." Doc stood up and began clearing the table. "Think you can persuade Sparky to help Teddy feed the chickens, the rabbits, and the duck?"

"I will if I can catch them!" Val was about to leave the kitchen when their cat, Cleveland, who had been sitting on the counter next to the cookie tin, jumped to the floor with a solid *flump!* He peered up at her with huge yellow eyes.

"Rrraow?" he cried. Val leaned down to stroke his head.

"Okay, Cleveland — I haven't forgotten about you. I'll feed you in a minute, I promise. Erin, I'll take care of the dishes."

"Anybody home?" Jill stuck her blonde head in the doorway. "Oh, hi, Dr. Taylor, hi, Erin — hi, Val. The door was open so I just came right in." Her eye was caught by the cookie tin. "Oh, wow! Mrs. Racer baked today, right? Can I have — whatever it is?"

Doc grinned. "Help yourself, Jill. It's brownies."

"Terrific!" Jill lifted the lid and took out a brownie. "I didn't have time for dessert because I wanted to get over here real fast. When's the big meeting you called me about?"

"As soon as Teddy and Sparky do their chores and I do mine," Val said. "While I stack the dishwasher, why don't you try to corral those two wild Indians?"

"Okay," Jill said through a mouthful of brownie. "Back in a flash!"

Fifteen minutes later, the Taylors, Sparky, and Jill were gathered in the living room. Doc said, "I hereby call this meeting to order. As you all know, Animal Inn's new boarding facility is going to open in four weeks, and we want to celebrate the opening with a big party. The purpose of this meeting is to decide who we're going to invite, what we're going to feed them, and who's going to be in charge of what."

Val raised her hand. When Doc nodded at her,

16

she said, "I think we should invite every client of Animal Inn and their pets."

"*All* of them?" Jill said. "Even Sadie, Mr. Pollard's prize sow, and all the horses and cows?"

"No," Doc put in quickly. "We have to draw the line somewhere, so I suggest we limit our animal guests to those under three feet high."

"Sadie's under three feet high," Teddy pointed out.

Doc stroked his short, graying beard. "You're right, Teddy. Okay, no animals more than three feet high or weighing more than three hundred pounds."

"Does that mean I can bring my cat, Charlie?" Sparky asked.

"Absolutely — provided he doesn't weigh more than three hundred pounds," Doc said with a perfectly straight face. "The last time I saw Charlie, he was getting pretty fat."

Sparky giggled. "He's not *that* fat!"

Teddy poked her in the ribs. "But *you* will be, if you don't stop eating Mrs. Racer's brownies. Hey, Dad, what about *people* who weigh more than three hundred pounds?"

"I do *not* weigh that much, Teddy Taylor!" Sparky yelled, pouncing on him. "I'll tickle you to death unless you take it back!"

"All right, you two," Doc said mildly. "If you'd

rather go outside and play instead of plan this party that's perfectly all right with me."

Teddy and Sparky looked at each other. Then Teddy sat down on the floor next to Jocko, and Sparky sat on the couch beside Erin, reaching out to pat Cleveland who was curled up in Erin's lap.

Doc smiled. "That's better. Now suppose we forget about the animals for the moment and concentrate on our human guests. What do you think we should feed them?"

"Mrs. Racer's cookies!" Teddy said promptly.

"And her brownies," Sparky added.

"And some of her wonderful shoo-fly pies," Erin said.

"Schnitz pies, too," Jill put in. "I love those little turnover things with the apple filling."

"Hey, wait a minute, gang," Val said. "At this rate, poor Mrs. Racer will be baking every minute from now until the party!"

"That's okay with me." Teddy rubbed his stomach. "Then we can have lots of samples."

Doc bent down and rumpled Teddy's golden-brown curls. "Now who's being piggy?" he asked, and Teddy made a face. "Vallie's right — we can't dump all the work on Mrs. Racer. And we can't have only desserts. What about real food?"

18

"My mom makes a really delicious bean pot," Jill said. "She uses dried limas, onions, green peppers, and lots of molasses and ketchup and stuff. We'll bring that."

"And my mom's potato salad is the best," Sparky said. "I bet she'd make gallons of it for the party."

Erin, who had been writing everything down, looked up and said, "Vallie and I can bake a ham and a turkey. Not even Vallie can foul that up!"

Val pretended to scowl at her sister. "Are you trying to say I'm not a fantastic cook?"

"Well, let's just say that when it comes to cooking meat, you're a great veterinarian!" Erin giggled at her own joke. "You don't have to eat it, you know — all you have to do is give me a hand in the kitchen."

"I think I can handle it," Val said. "But it seems to me that since we're celebrating the opening of a boarding kennel that cares for animals, it's kind of weird to *serve* animals to our guests."

"*You're* weird," Teddy said from the floor, where he was tussling with Jocko while Sunshine watched, wagging his plumy tail. "*Normal* people like to eat meat."

Val frowned at him. "How would you like to eat Jocko or Sunshine? In some parts of the world, people eat dogs the way *you* eat ham and turkey.''

"That's different — '' Teddy began, but Doc cut him off.

"We're talking about Essex, Pennsylvania, not Asia. If Vallie doesn't want to eat meat, that's her decision. At least she's willing to help Erin prepare the meat, and I appreciate that. We all have to respect each other's point of view." He turned to Jill. "Can we count on you to provide some of your special popcorn, Jill?''

"Oh, sure," Jill said. "Dad brought home a new popper the other day. It's much bigger than the old one, so I can make tons!''

Erin looked at her list. "I think we have enough food now. But what about something to drink?''

Doc solemnly raised his hand. "Since I'm a champion lemonade maker, I'll volunteer to provide plenty of it, if Teddy will help me squeeze the lemons.''

Teddy said he would, and Val added, "I haven't asked Toby yet, but I'm sure his dad would donate lots of ice cream from their shops. Let's ask him to do that instead of letting us all pig out at the ice cream parlor for free like you suggested!''

"Good idea, Vallie." Doc smiled at her. "Would you handle that?''

"I'll ask Toby about it tomorrow morning," Val

said. "After Erin and I go to the farmers' market."

In Essex, there was a market house where the local farmers came every Thursday and Saturday to sell their produce. It wasn't at all like the supermarkets in the shopping centers, which carried food in boxes, cans, or wrapped in plastic. At the farmers' market, everything was fresh and natural. Fruits and vegetables were home grown, meats were butchered on the farms, and baked goods had been taken out of the ovens only an hour or so before they were displayed for sale. People came to the Essex Farmers' Market from as far away as Baltimore and Philadelphia, because they loved seeing the Amish and Mennonite families in their traditional garb as much as they enjoyed the delicious food.

"I don't have to come, do I?" Teddy asked. "Me and Sparky was gonna play soccer with Eric and Billy and the gang."

Erin arched her eyebrows. "Sparky and *I* were going to play soccer."

"Hey, you want to play, too?" Teddy said. "Then who's gonna go to the market with Vallie?"

Doc groaned. "Erin was just correcting your grammar, Teddy. You should have said, 'Sparky and *I* were going to play soccer with the gang.' You're in third grade — haven't you learned anything?"

"I sure have," Teddy said, grinning. "Me and

21

Billy and Eric and Sparky have learned a whole lot about soccer!"

Val laughed. "Dad, I think you'd better give up. Teddy's hopeless! But we still have a lot to talk about, like what we're going to feed our animal guests, and who's going to send out the invitations."

"My friend Alison and I can do the invitations. She's a good artist. But we can't do them until you decide on a date and a time," Jill said.

Resting her notebook on top of Cleveland, Erin flipped to the back, where she had pasted in a small calendar. "Let's see — how about Saturday, the tenth of June, Daddy?"

Doc nodded. "Sounds good. We'll close Animal Inn early that day, and the party can start at four."

"Dad, I just thought of something," Val said. "Isn't that the day of the Humane Society's dog show?"

"No," Doc said. "The dog show is Sunday, the eleventh. We were discussing it last night at our monthly board meeting. The tenth will be just fine. Now, about those invitations. . . ."

By the time they had worked out the rest of the details, it was almost eight o'clock. Suddenly the doorbell rang.

"I'll get it," Val said. When she opened the door,

she saw Mrs. Sparks standing outside under a bright pink umbrella.

"Hi, Val," Sparky's mother said. "Since it's raining, I thought I'd pick Sparky up rather than making her bike home. She can get her bike tomorrow, if that's all right."

"Oh, sure. What's one bike more or less?" Val said cheerfully. "Come on in, Mrs. Sparks. *Down*, Jocko! *Down*, Sunshine!" she added to the dogs, who were jumping up and down and barking to welcome the visitor. "I'm sorry — they're just excited."

"That's all right. I don't mind," Mrs. Sparks said. "I won't come any further," she said, "or I'll track mud all over the rug. Just tell Sparky I'm here, will you, Val?"

As Mrs. Sparks leaned down to pat the dogs, Val thought how pretty she was. Not as pretty as her own mother had been, of course, but nice and healthy-looking with her pink cheeks and her windblown hair. Mrs. Sparks worked as a paralegal for a law firm in Essex, and every other time Val had seen her, she had been wearing a tailored dress or suit. In jeans, sneakers, and a yellow windbreaker, she looked like a different person.

Apparently Doc thought so, too, because when he came out into the hall to see who had arrived, he looked puzzled.

23

"It's Mrs. Sparks, Dad. She's come to pick up Sparky," Val told him on her way into the living room. "Sparky, your mom's here."

"Nuts!" Sparky trotted into the hall. "Mom, do I *have* to go home now? Teddy and I were going to go play with his hamsters."

"Sorry, honey — it's pretty late," Mrs. Sparks said. "You're going to be playing together tomorrow, so you need a good night's sleep." She smiled at Doc. "Thanks for feeding my little girl tonight. I hope she didn't eat you out of house and home."

"She tried!" Teddy said, pulling one of Sparky's pigtails again.

"That's enough, Teddy," Doc said quickly. "Always a pleasure having Sparky here. You might be interested in knowing she volunteered your famous potato salad for Animal Inn's party next month."

Mrs. Sparks looked surprised. "She did?"

"You'll do it, won't you?" Sparky said. "I'll help peel the potatoes, honest. It's going to be a terrific party, with people and animals and — "

"Suppose you tell me about it on the way home," Mrs. Sparks cut in. "Now say good night to everybody. Teddy, you plan on having lunch with us tomorrow, okay?"

"Okay." Teddy took Cleveland from Sparky and

draped the cat over his shoulder. "See ya later, alligator," he said to Sparky.

"In a while, crocodile," she sang out.

"You really don't have to make that potato salad, you know," Doc said, smiling. "You're invited anyway."

Mrs. Sparks laughed. "I accept with pleasure. And I'll be delighted to make whatever you need. I don't think I've ever been to a party for people *and* animals before!"

"Come to think of it, neither have I. What have I gotten myself into?" Doc shook his head and laughed.

Chapter
3

The next morning, Doc dropped Teddy at his friend Eric's house, then swung by the market and let Val and Erin out.

"I'll probably get to Animal Inn around eleven, Dad," Val told him.

"Have a good day, Daddy. Don't work too hard," Erin said, kissing her father on the cheek. "After Vallie and I get back, I'll be going to ballet class, and then I'm going over to Olivia's. We're going to have lunch and watch *The Red Shoes* on her VCR. I'll be home in plenty of time to get supper."

"See you later, girls."

Doc drove off in the van, and Val and Erin, each with a market basket over her arm, went into the big old building. Even though it was barely nine o'clock, the market was filled with people wandering from stall to stall.

Val hadn't been to the market in months because she was usually too busy at Animal Inn. Now she looked all around, savoring the sights and smells. "It hasn't changed one bit," she said. "Remember when Mother used to bring us here? She always brought each of us a big soft pretzel."

Erin nodded. "Yes — and those delicious crab cakes at Miller's, and the pepper slaw she liked so much. . . ."

"And remember the time Teddy tried to eat the Indian corn and Mother got so scared because she thought he'd swallowed some of it? I think he must have been about four. . . ."

The sisters were silent for a moment, remembering their beautiful, loving mother. Neither Val, Erin, nor Teddy spoke about her very much, but they all thought about her a lot. Val knew that deep inside, they would never stop missing her.

Val stuck a hand in the pocket of her denim jacket and pulled out the list. "You've got the money right?"

Erin held up her wallet. "Sure do. Okay, let's get started."

"Bread first," Val said. "Did you say Staub's?"

"Nope — Geiselman's is where Mrs. Racer goes. It's right over there, next to the Pollard Pork Products stand."

Val couldn't look at the display of sausages, hams, and chops at Pollard's. Mr. Pollard was a very nice man, but Val had become friends with many of his Pork Products while they were still walking around. Fortunately Mr. Pollard was busy with a customer, so he didn't see her hurry by.

"Best pigs' feet in the county, Mrs. Crist," she heard him say. Val shuddered.

"What do you think, Vallie? Whole wheat or rye?" Erin asked.

"Whole wheat," Val replied. "Why don't you give me some money, and I'll buy some cheese while you get the sausage?"

Val was waiting while the smiling Amish girl at the cheese stand cut and weighed a piece of sharp cheddar, when Mrs. Myers, one of Doc's clients, bustled over to her. Mrs. Myers was a small, birdlike woman in her early sixties, and she usually had a cheerful word for everyone. Her Pekingese, Ling-ling, was a frequent visitor to Animal Inn — not because he was often sick, but because Mrs. Myers was a worry-wart about her beloved Peke. Today she was very upset.

"Oh, Vallie, the most *terrible* thing has happened!" she cried. "I just don't know *what* I'm going to do!"

"Is it Ling-ling's tummy again?" Val asked sympathetically.

Mrs. Myers shook her neat gray head. "No —

28

it's not his *inside* this time, it's his *outside*!''

''Mange?'' Val suggested.

Offended at the very idea, Mrs. Myers exclaimed, ''Of course not! But he'll probably *get* mange, or something even *worse* now that Ida Potter's closing The Pink Poodle!''

The Pink Poodle was the town's one and only pet grooming salon, and Val was sure that Mrs. Myers's Ling-ling was probably one of Ida's regular customers. ''That's too bad, Mrs. Myers,'' she said politely. ''I hadn't heard about it.''

''It's a *tragedy*, that's what it is,'' Mrs. Myers moaned. ''Ida's taken it into her head to retire and move to *Florida*, of all places! Irresponsible, that's what she is, just plain irresponsible. How is my darling Lingy going to get his weekly shampoo and blow-dry if Ida leaves town? He'll get all tangled and matted and *dirty!* And I'm not the only one who's upset. Just about every pet owner in Essex is *devastated!*''

Val privately doubted that, but said only, ''Well, I guess people will just have to start washing and grooming their own animals. We do it all the time. Neither Jocko nor Sunshine have ever been taken to The Pink Poodle, and they're in pretty good shape.''

''Yes, but *your* dogs aren't — er, they're not pedigreed, like Lingy. You see, Vallie dear, pedi-

29

greed puppy dogs need very special, delicate treatment. Oh, what am I going to do?"

"Is something the matter, Mrs. Myers?" Erin asked, coming up beside Val.

"Ida Potter's closing The Pink Poodle and moving to Florida, so Ling-ling won't be able to get his weekly beauty treatment," Val told her, trying hard not to smile.

"Gee, that's a pity," Erin said sincerely. "Does Ling-ling know?"

"I haven't told him yet," Mrs. Myers said with a sigh. "But when I do, I'm sure he'll be just *miserable*. Oh, there's Maybella Wentworth — she takes Princess Tuptim, her prize Siamese, to The Pink Poodle, too. I wonder if she's heard the awful news. . . ." Picking up her basket, she hurried off. "Yoo-hoo — Maybella! The most *dreadful* thing. . . ."

Val and Erin looked at each other, and when they were sure Mrs. Myers was far enough away they both broke up.

"Imagine getting all bent out of shape because your dog's beauty parlor is closing," Val giggled.

"People get pretty weird about their pets, don't they?" Erin said.

"Do they ever! Especially people like Mrs. Myers and Mrs. Wentworth. But I can understand why. Their pets are almost like children to them."

"I guess everybody needs someone to love," Erin mused, "even if it's only a little animated mop like Ling-ling."

"A *purebred* animated mop," Val said. " 'Pedigreed puppy dogs need very special treatment.' " She made a face. "Oh, well, we'd better get the rest of our marketing done, or I'll never make it to work by eleven, and you'll be late for your ballet class."

By the time the girls had finished buying all the items on Mrs. Racer's list (and two big soft pretzels for themselves) it was after ten o'clock, and their baskets felt as if they weighed a ton.

They had gone only half a block down Market Street when they heard a car horn. Val looked up. An old blue sedan was pulling up beside them.

"Looks like you girls could use a lift," said the woman who was driving. It was Donna Hartman, Ida Potter's assistant at The Pink Poodle.

"Thanks, Donna. We sure could," Val said.

"Then hop right in. Erin, you get in the back. But watch out for the door — it's hard to open and even harder to close."

After Erin and Val were seated, Val said, "So what are you going to do now that The Pink Poodle's closing?"

31

Donna glanced over at her with a wry smile. "You heard about that, huh? I'm not surprised. News travels fast in this town." She ran a hand through her frizzy blonde curls and pursed her bright red lips. Donna always wore lots of makeup, and Val noticed that her hair resembled the poodles she groomed. "Well, Vallie, I'll tell you the truth. I don't really know. It was a big shock to me when Ida told me she was retiring. She asked me if I'd like to take over the Poodle and run it myself, but I don't have a head for business like Ida does. Besides, I can't afford to buy her out." She shook her head sadly. "I guess maybe I'll do a little grooming on the side every now and then, but I'll have to get another job. Jim and I can't make it on his salary alone."

"You'd better turn here, or you're going to miss our street," Erin told her from the backseat.

"Thanks. With all I have on my mind, it's a wonder I don't run right into a telephone pole." Donna made the turn onto Princess Street, narrowly missing two old ladies, who shook their fists at her in unison. "Sorry!" Donna yelled.

"We were talking to Mrs. Myers at the market," Val said. "She's real upset about the Poodle closing."

"Her and a lot of other folks. You know, Vallie, it's important how animals look. Grooming isn't as important as what your dad does for them. But there's a lot of folks who don't know how to keep their animals clean and tidy, and they need help. Then there's those with fancy show dogs that need special clips. You'd be surprised at all the different kinds of clipping I do — *used* to do." Donna turned onto Old Mill Road and slowed to a stop in front of the Taylors' house. "Well, here we are. Take care, now. Next time you see me, I might be working in the pet department of Woolworth's. I put in an application yesterday. Need any help with those baskets?"

Val and Erin assured her that they could manage just fine, and Donna drove off, waving to them from the window.

"Poor Donna!" Erin said as she and Val lugged their baskets up the front walk. "I feel so sorry she lost her job, don't you?"

"Yes, I do," Val said. "I don't think she's going to be very happy working at the dime store. She really loves grooming animals, and everyone says she's very good at it — even Lila Bascombe. Her mother takes Marie Antoinette, Lila's miniature poodle, to The Pink Poodle all the time. Lila's going to have a fit when she finds out it's closing. But then, she's always having a fit about something." Lila Bascombe, who was in Val's class at junior high, was not one of her favorite people.

The girls went inside and began putting away

the food. "You know," Val said, "I always thought a beauty parlor for pets was pretty silly. But what Donna said makes sense. It *is* important for animals to be clean and look nice, and their owners aren't always able to do a good job. I guess The Pink Poodle *does* do something important."

Erin said, "Lila may be a pain, but Marie Antoinette looks so adorable when she's just been clipped, with a cute little bow on her topknot and her toenails painted pink." She looked down at their dogs. "I wonder how Jocko would look with a bow in his hair?"

"Ridiculous!" Val said promptly, but she couldn't help smiling at the thought of the shaggy little black-and-white mongrel all decked out in ribbons and bows like a birthday present.

"I wish there were something we could do for Donna," Erin said with a sigh.

"Me, too. . . ." Suddenly Val had a thought. "Maybe there *is* something we can do!"

"What do you mean?" Erin asked.

"Well, some veterinary clinics have grooming facilities along with everything else. And Animal Inn is going to have a lot more room when the new wing is finished. I wonder if Dad would consider hiring Donna now that The Pink Poodle is going out of business?"

"Oh, Vallie, that's a neat idea!" Erin exclaimed. "Why don't you ask him about it today?"

"I just might do that," Val said. "It certainly wouldn't hurt to ask."

Erin glanced at the kitchen clock. "Uh-oh — it's a quarter to eleven. I'd better get going, or I'll be late for ballet class and Miss Tamara will have a conniption!"

"You go ahead. I'll put the rest of the stuff away." Val grinned. "I don't think my boss will fire me if I don't make it to work right on the dot."

"Thanks, Vallie!" Erin grabbed her ballet bag and ran out the back door, her long blonde ponytail flying.

As Val rescued the cheese from Cleveland, who was sniffing at the waxed paper wrapping, she wondered how her father would react to the idea of hiring Donna. She had a feeling he just might go for it. Then she thought about Toby. He'd probably tell her she was out of her mind. She could hear him now: "A beauty parlor at Animal Inn? Have you lost your marbles or something?"

35

Chapter
4

"A beauty parlor at Animal Inn? Have you lost your marbles or something?" Toby squawked when Val told him what she had in mind.

Val sighed. "That's exactly what I thought you'd say. Are you going to give Fluffy Henderson his pills, or do you want me to do it?"

Toby opened Fluffy's cage and took out the furry black cat. "I'll do it. I have his medication right here." Tucking Fluffy under his left arm, Toby popped two small yellow pills into the cat's open mouth, then stroked Fluffy's throat to make sure he swallowed them both. "There you go, Fluff," he said. "That oughta take care of any worms you have left."

The cat gave him a dirty look as Toby put him back into his cage and sat down and began to wash.

Val consulted her chart. "Okay, that does it for all the animals in the infirmary. Pat's leaving for the day, so I'll take over the reception desk while you have lunch. Since I came in late, I'm not taking a lunch break."

Toby followed her out of the infirmary, one end of which was draped with a big sheet of plastic to separate it from the area where construction was going on. The workers were having lunch, so for the moment it was quiet.

"You've got to be kidding," Toby said. "This is a veterinary clinic, not a place where animals get all prettied up!"

"I know that. But a lot of our clients depend on The Pink Poodle to wash their pets because they don't know how to do it themselves." Val pushed open the door to the reception room, Toby at her heels. "Hi, Pat," she said to the plump little woman behind the desk. "I'm here — you can leave now."

Pat Dempwolf stood up and began struggling into her sweater. "Not too many appointments today, Vallie," she said. "But I took lots of reservations for the boarding kennel! I wrote them all down in the red book to keep them separate from Doc's regular appointments in the blue book. Hey, Toby, what's wrong? You don't look too happy."

Toby mumbled something, but the only words that were clear were "beauty parlor."

"Yes, that's right — I'm going to the beauty par-

37

lor," Pat said cheerfully. "How did you know? My perm's just about grown out. Well, Vallie, you tell Doc I'll be here bright and early Tuesday morning, same as usual. Have a nice day, now."

She picked up her huge pocketbook and trotted out, smiling and waving to the people who were sitting in the waiting room with their cats and dogs.

Val took her place behind the reception desk and opened the red book. "Gee, look at that! July's almost all booked up," she said to Toby.

"Have you talked to Doc yet about this idea of yours?" he asked.

"Not yet. I haven't had the chance — he's been busy with his patients ever since I arrived."

"Well, I think you're bananas, and I bet he will, too."

Val scowled at him. "Toby, Donna's a really talented groomer, and she's a nice person, too. She needs a job, and there are people in this town who need *her*."

"Oh, sure," Toby said sarcastically. "People really *need* to take their dogs to a beauty parlor! We've got lots of dogs on the farm, and they'd *die* of embarrassment if we did something like that to them. And that's another thing," he went on before Val could say anything. "Wait till my brothers find

out I'm working at a place that has a beauty parlor —
they'll laugh themselves sick!"

"Excuse me, Vallie," said a fashionably dressed
woman with a cat carrier on the bench next to her.
"But Tiger and I have been waiting for a very long
time. Will you please inform your father that I have
a Women's Club meeting at one-thirty, and he must
examine Tiger in the next fifteen minutes or I'll be
late." It wasn't really a question, but a command.

Val quickly opened Doc's blue appointment
book and glanced at Saturday's page. "Well, Mrs.
Desmond, according to this he's treating Hank Snyder's guinea pig, Squeaky, for mites. Squeaky
Snyder's appointment was for twelve-thirty, so he
ought to be finished any minute now."

Mrs. Desmond sniffed haughtily. "I certainly
hope so. Poor Tiger is very uncomfortable — he's
been scratching for days, and his poor neck is all
raw and bleeding."

"Maybe he's got fleas," Toby suggested, trying
to be helpful.

Mrs. Desmond stiffened. *"Fleas? My* cat? Impossible! He wears a flea collar, and I dust him with
flea powder every single day. No, I'm sure it's some
obscure skin condition. Tiger has very sensitive
skin."

"Yeeoow," Tiger added from his carrier.

"If Squeaky Snyder isn't out here in the next five minutes, I'll buzz Dad on the intercom," Val promised. Then she turned back to Toby. "I wish you'd stop talking about beauty parlors. A grooming facility does more than make animals look pretty. Like Dad always says, a clean animal is almost always a healthy animal, and some folks need help in keeping their animals clean."

Just then the door to the treatment room opened, and Hank Snyder, a tall, gangly young man, came out with a cardboard box clutched to his chest.

"Thanks, Doc," he called over his shoulder. "I'll use that insecticide you gave me and I'm sure Squeaky'll be feeling a lot better."

Hank paid his bill as Doc stuck his head out and smiled at Mrs. Desmond. "Tiger's next," he said. "Women's Club today, right? We'll have you out of here in no time flat."

Beaming, Mrs. Desmond picked up Tiger's cat carrier and bustled into the treatment room.

"Dad, have you heard that The Pink Poodle is closing?" Val asked about an hour later, as Doc wolfed down a couple of home-cured ham and Swiss cheese sandwiches she and Erin had bought for him at the market.

Doc nodded. When he had swallowed, he said, "Everybody's talking about it. Too bad."

The workers were hammering again, so Val had to shout. "That means Donna Hartman's out of a job."

"I know," Doc said. "Any pickles?"

Val passed him a big fat one. "Dad, I was thinking . . ."

"So was I." Doc bit into the pickle. "Mmm — nice and sour." He munched for a moment, then went on, "I wouldn't be surprised if we've both been thinking the same thing. My thought was that since we're expanding Animal Inn, it might be a good idea to add a grooming service. And now that Donna's going to be out of a job. . . ."

Val's face lit up. "That's exactly *my* idea! Oh, Dad, are you going to hire her? Donna gave Erin and me a ride home from the market this morning, and she was telling us that she might have to start working at the dime store or somewhere like that because they can't make out on Jim's salary alone. And that would really be too bad, because everybody says she's a really good groomer, and she loves animals, and — "

"Whoa!" Doc grinned at her. "You don't have to convince me. It was my idea, remember?"

41

Val laughed. "Mine, too! Guess I'm just a chip off the old block, huh?"

"You are indeed." He wadded up the waxed paper that had wrapped his sandwiches and tossed it into the waste basket. Standing up, he brushed a few crumbs from the white coat he wore over his T-shirt and jeans. Then he gave her a hug. "Okay, Val — I'll give Donna a call tonight when we get home. And in the meantime, I'd better get back to work. Who's our next patient?"

"Mr. Brumbaugh's Irish setter," Val said promptly. "Colleen's puppies are due any day now, and Mr. Brumbaugh wants to make sure everything's okay. I'll tell Toby to send them in." On her way to the waiting room, she suddenly thought of something. "By the way, Dad, what was the matter with Tiger Desmond? Why has he been scratching himself?"

Scrubbing his hands at the sink, Doc said, "Flea powder."

"Flea *powder*? Not fleas?"

"Right. Mrs. Desmond's been overdoing it with the flea powder. She sprinkles that poor cat every day. Tiger's developed an allergy to the stuff. I told her to rely on Tiger's flea collar to take care of any possible fleas, and gave her some medication for the allergy. Tiger's going to be just fine, and I'm sure

Mrs. Desmond was right on time for her Women's Club meeting."

Smiling, Val went into the reception area, where Mr. Brumbaugh and Colleen were waiting. Colleen's silky red body, usually so slim, was bulging with the puppies she was about to deliver. But she was perfectly calm, unlike her owner. Mr. Brumbaugh was a nervous wreck. The minute he saw Val, he jumped to his feet, clutching Colleen's lead.

"It's about time!" he said, in a squawk that was completely unlike his normal deep voice. "Toby told me that Doc was having lunch, and I can understand that. Everybody has to eat lunch! But Colleen's going to have her first litter, and she's a very high-strung dog!"

Colleen looked up at her master, then at Val, and wagged her plumy tail.

Val bent down and stroked the dog's head. "Doc's ready to see you now," she said, more to the dog than to Mr. Brumbaugh. "Don't worry about a thing. Everything's going to be just fine."

"A lot you know," Mr. Brumbaugh blustered, heading for the treatment room. "You're just a kid! What do you know about things like this?"

From behind the reception desk, Toby said, "Val knows a whole lot. She's been helping her father take care of animals for years! If she says everything's going to be okay, then everything's going to be okay."

Val gave him a grateful glance. "Thanks, Toby," she said. And very formally she added, "The doctor will examine Colleen. He doesn't anticipate any problems."

Muttering under his breath, Mr. Brumbaugh led Colleen into the treatment room. When the door had closed behind him, Toby said, "Did you talk to your father about the beauty parlor?"

Val smiled sweetly. "Yes, I did. And he thinks it's a terrific idea. He's going to call Donna tonight."

Toby groaned. "Swell! I won't be able to show my face at home or anywhere else! Everybody's going to say that I'm some kind of a hairdresser for dogs!"

"Oh, cut it out, Toby!" Val sighed. "You won't have to do any grooming at all. And I keep telling you, it's *not* just a beauty parlor."

As Val took his seat behind the desk, Toby said, "Well, I guess maybe you're right. But I still think it's a goofy idea." He headed for the door. "Gotta go check on that cow in the Large Animal Clinic, the one with the ringworm. It's almost time for her medication. If there's one thing I know about, it's cows. And cows," he added just before he left, "*don't* go to beauty parlors!"

* * *

44

"Hey, Vallie, what's this Toby's been tellin' me about Doc turnin' this place into a beauty parlor?" Mike Strickler asked a few hours later. Mike was Animal Inn's night man and looked after Doc's patients on Sundays and Mondays when the clinic was closed. Small, wiry, and bow-legged, he reminded Val of a Pennsylvania Dutch leprechaun. Nobody knew exactly how old Mike was, but he liked to say he was somewhere between ninety-two and a hundred and twelve. Now his faded blue eyes twinkled under the visor of his scruffy baseball cap as he grinned at Val. "Gonna give all them cats and dogs a permanent wave?"

Val frowned at him. "Oh, Mike, not you, too! If *you're* going to start, you and Toby will drive me right up the wall!"

"Now, now — don't get all *ferhoodled*," Mike said, leaning on the handle of his push broom. "I was just teasin', Vallie. Can't you take a tease anymore?"

Val smiled apologetically. "Sure I can. It's just that Toby's making such a big deal out of Dad asking Donna Hartman to work here now that The Pink Poodle's closing. Did you know about that, Mike?"

"About Ida Potter retirin' to Florida so's she can be close to her kids and grandkids? Yep, I know, all right. Though why she's retirin', young as she is, beats me." Mike began sweeping the empty waiting room. "Why, Ida can't be more than sixty-nine, give or take a couple o' years. A real spring chicken, that's what Ida is. Now when *I* was sixty-nine, I was hardly dry behind the ears! I'm not gonna start thinkin' about retirin' until I'm at least a hundred and twenty-three."

"Good!" Val said, laughing. "Because I don't know what we'd do without you."

"As for Doc hirin' Donna, I'm all in favor of it," Mike said. "Give the place some class, know what I mean? Not that it ain't got class now," he added quickly. "But I bet once she's gussyin' up some of them fancy dogs, the ones that go to that high-society vet over in Harrisburg. . . ."

"Dr. Callahan?"

"That's the one. Well, once them society dogs start comin' here to get their shampoos and their toenails painted and such, it'll only be a matter of time before they're comin' here when they got a runny nose or need some shots. Doc Taylor's the best vet in these parts, only the society folks don't think so 'cause he don't charge the earth, and sometimes he don't charge at all if he knows folks can't pay. But they'll come around, you mark my words, Vallie. Yessiree, they'll come around."

"Thanks, Mike. I think so, too." Val beamed at

the old man. "And now I'm going to see The Ghost. I haven't even said hello to him today because we've been so busy. If I hurry, I'll have time for a ride before supper."

"You know, Ghost, Mike's right," Val said to the big dapple-gray gelding as they ambled along a country lane. "The people who take their pets to Dr. Callahan are the same people who use The Pink Poodle. Oh, some of our clients go there, too, and they're the ones I'm really interested in. But if Dad hires Donna, Dr. Callahan's patients just might start coming to Dad, and it would be great to expand his practice."

The Ghost flicked his ears back and forth the way he always did whenever Val spoke to him.

"I have to admit that even though I've never met Dr. Callahan, I don't like him very much. Mr. Merrill was going to tell him to destroy you because you couldn't jump anymore. And he'd have done it, too! I'm so glad he wasn't available."

The Ghost snorted and nodded his head in agreement.

"I just wish Toby didn't think the whole idea was so silly. I have to find a way to convince him that a grooming facility isn't just primping and prettying, or else he's going to be absolutely impossible.

And Toby's one of my very best friends, so I'd hate to be arguing with him all the time. . . . " Val looked at her watch. "Oops — it's almost time for supper. If we don't turn back right away, I'll be late. But we'll have a nice, long ride tomorrow, I promise. I'll do my homework real early, and then I'll spend the rest of the day with you."

Pricking up his ears, the Ghost began trotting back down the road to Animal Inn.

Chapter
5

Donna was overjoyed at Doc's offer of a job. They agreed that Animal Inn would buy all of Ida's grooming equipment and that Donna would set up her grooming operation in Animal Inn's old isolation ward one week later. Because the ward had a separate entrance, people could take their pets there without having to wait in the clinic's reception room. First thing Monday morning, Doc took out an ad in the local paper, stating that Donna Hartman, formerly of The Pink Poodle, would be continuing to provide her services at Animal Inn as part of the expanded animal care program the clinic was now offering its clients.

When Val showed up for work on Tuesday after school, she saw that Pat had put the ad up on the bulletin board behind the reception desk, right next to an old article the paper had run about Doc's and Val's heroism in rescuing injured animals during the big fire at the Humane Society's shelter.

"You wouldn't *believe* how many calls we've gotten about that ad!" Pat said happily. "Between the boarding kennel and the pet grooming salon, the phone's been ringing off the hook."

"Terrific!" Val said. "Is Toby here yet? I've been doing a lot of reading over the past couple of days, and I want to tell him what I've found out."

"I think he's helping Doc with Frank Neilson's basset hound — poor Wrinkles has another ear infection. Oh, Vallie, could you cover the desk for a few minutes while I go take some aspirin? Those workers have been hammering all day long, and I've got a terrible headache!"

Val took over until Pat returned and Toby came out of the treatment room with Wrinkles. When he had delivered the basset to its owner and Wrinkles had waddled off with Mr. Neilson, Val said, "Toby, I have to talk to you."

"If it's about the beauty parlor, I don't want to hear about it," Toby mumbled. "Besides, Doc needs you to help him with Killer. He says you're the only one who can make that dog stand still for an examination. Catch you later, okay?"

Val shrugged. "Okay." She went over to Mr. Williamson, who was sitting on a chair with his tiny Yorkshire terrier on his lap. The Yorkie was wearing a doll-sized T-shirt with KILLER printed across the chest, and the hair on the top of his head was caught up in a blue plastic barrette. Killer greeted Val with delighted yips as she scooped him up with one hand. "This won't take long, Mr. Williamson," she told the dog's owner and hurried into the treatment room, giggling as the Yorkie licked her face.

After Doc had finished his examination, giving Killer a clean bill of health, Val tracked Toby down in the infirmary. While she helped him give the animals their medicine, she said, "I guess you're still all bent out of shape about the grooming thing, aren't you?"

"I am *not* bent out of shape. It just seems dumb, that's all. I mean, what's the point of cutting poddles' hair so they look like — like *freaks*?" Toby opened the door of a tan-and-black mongrel's cage and checked the bandage on the dog's front leg. "Now *this*," he said, "is a *dog*, not some kind of dopey toy!"

"I bet you don't know anything about poodles, do you?" Val asked. "Well, I didn't either until I started doing some research in Dad's books. Did you know that poodles were hunting dogs for hundreds of years?"

"*Hunting* dogs? *Poodles?*"

"That's right. They were used for duck hunting. That's why their hindquarters were clipped

51

smooth — so they could swim more easily. The fur on their chest was left long and thick to keep them warm when they went hunting in the winter. The hunters used to tie bright-colored ribbons to their heads and tails so they could keep track of the dogs when they went after ducks in marshes and ponds. Poodles are great retrievers, and they love water. That's how they got their name — from the German word for 'puddle.' So it's not all that silly. It's traditional.''

"Retrievers, huh?" Toby looked interested. Then he added, "But I bet they didn't paint their toenails and stuff like that way back then!"

"No," Val admitted. "I don't imagine they did. And I agree with you — that's pretty silly. But you and I won't have to do it. That'll be Donna's job. You'll be nice to her, won't you?" she asked anxiously. "You won't make fun of her or anything?"

Toby looked offended. "What do you take me for? Of course I'll be nice to her. She's a friend of Doc's and yours, and you're my friends, so I guess she'll be my friend, too — just so long as I don't have to help out with the beauty parlor!"

"You won't," Val assured him, smiling. "Except . . ."

"Except what?" Toby asked suspiciously.

"Well, Dad wants us to paint the old isolation

ward so it'll be all nice and fresh when Donna moves in. You wouldn't mind doing that, would you?"

"No, I guess not. I'm good at painting." He thought a minute. "What color? *Not* pink!"

"No, not pink. I was thinking about a bright, sunny yellow — Mrs. Racer has some yellow and white fabric that she's going to use to make curtains. Think you can handle yellow?"

Toby nodded. "Any color's okay except pink. I don't want to walk around with pink paint splattered all over my jeans."

"Good," Val said. "Maybe Dad and I can get the paint tonight on our way home. Then if we don't have too many patients tomorrow afternoon, you and I can put on the first coat."

By Thursday Animal Inn's new grooming salon was a cheerful shade of yellow — and so were Val and Toby's work clothes. On Saturday Mrs. Racer arrived at the Taylors' house bright and early with a pair of yellow-and-white checked gingham curtains for the room's one window. Even Toby had to admit that the old isolation ward looked pretty good. And when Donna's husband brought her and all her equipment over, Donna was delighted.

"Oh, Vallie, it's just beautiful!" she cried. "Isn't it beautiful, Jim?"

Jim, a husky redhead in grease-stained coveralls, nodded and grinned. "Sure is."

Even Toby agreed. He added, "I hope Mrs. Hartman's beauty parlor is a big success."

Jim threw back his head and laughed heartily. "Me, too! We didn't know how we were gonna manage now that Donna's expecting. But she can keep right on working till the baby's born, and that'll help out a lot."

"Oh, Donna, I didn't know!" Val exclaimed. "Congratulations! When is the baby due?"

"Oh, not till mid-October," Donna said, beaming. "And I intend to keep busy every minute. I'm so lucky to have this job! We're banking every cent so he or she can go to college when the time comes. You tell your dad that if it's a boy, we're going to name it after him! And if it's a girl, well, how would you like to be her godmother? Valentine Hartman sounds just right, don't you think? Valentine and hearts?"

Val felt herself blushing — she was sure her face was red. "I'd love it! I've never been a godmother before."

"But you've got a namesake," Toby reminded her.

"I do?"

"Sure. Remember when my kid brother Jake's

rabbit had babies? He named one of 'em after you, and now she's a mother herself.''

Amazed, Val said, ''Well, what do you know!'' Turning to Donna and Jim, she added, ''If you don't want to name your daughter after me *and* a rabbit, I'll understand.'' That made everybody laugh.

Toby and Val helped the Hartmans arrange the tools of Donna's trade — brushes, combs, clippers, shampoos, conditioners, and various bottles containing preparation for the animals' skin and hair — on the freshly painted shelves. Toby made a face when Donna began setting out an array of nail polishes on a little tray, but he didn't say anything. He also didn't comment when she produced several spools of bright-colored ribbons.

As Donna placed piles of fluffy towels on a shelf near the sink, Val told her about all the appointments she, Toby, and Pat had made, beginning on Tuesday morning.

''That's wonderful,'' Donna said happily. ''Ida was really worried that people would start taking their pets to Harrisburg, or maybe not have them groomed at all. She told me just yesterday that she wouldn't sleep right if she didn't know her friends were in good hands, especially the ones we cared for at home.''

''At home?'' Val asked.

''For the pets whose owners don't have cars or

are just too old or sick to bring them to The Pink Poodle. Ida and me made house calls, too, Vallie, just like you and Doc. Now you take Mathilda Reineman, for instance. Miss Mathilda's virtually housebound because of her arthritis. But she sets great store by her Pomeranian, Suzy, and Suzy's nothing but a ball of fluff that needs a shampoo once a month to keep her looking nice. Well, I drive out to Miss Mathilda's place and give Suzy the full treatment every single month, and Miss Mathilda always gives me a snack and a nice hot cup of tea when I'm done. She doesn't get many visitors and it makes her feel good to sit at the kitchen table with Suzy and me and hear all the latest gossip. I think Suzy likes it, too! Everybody needs somebody, know what I mean?"

Val nodded. "Yes, I do. Dad's always telling me that TLC is very important. That's Tender Loving Care," she added for Toby's benefit. "Do you think Miss Mathilda and Suzy would like to come to our party next month?" she asked Donna. "Mike could pick them up in the van. Come to think of it, he could pick up a lot of people who can't drive and their pets."

"I bet Miss Mathilda would love it," Donna said.

"Boy, Animal Inn's expanding, all right," Toby said. "A boarding kennel, another treatment room, a big infirmary, a beauty par — " Catching Val's eye,

56

he quickly substituted. "A grooming facility, and now a taxi service!"

"Only for one party," Val pointed out. "You're invited, too," she told Donna and Jim. "And Spotty, your Dalmation, of course. My friend Jill and I are going to send out the invitations next week."

"My dad's going to provide lots of ice cream and sugar cones and sprinkles," Toby added. "There'll be food for the animals, too."

Donna said, "I make a delicious cole slaw, if I say so myself. Should I bring some to the party?"

Val smiled. "That would be great! It's going to be the biggest and best party Essex has ever seen!"

After the Hartmans left Toby said to Val, "They're nice people. I guess it won't be too bad having Donna at Animal Inn."

Val wanted to say, "I told you so," but she didn't. She just waved as Toby mounted his bike for the ride back to the Currans' farm. "See you Tuesday!" she called as he pedaled away.

Chapter
6

On Tuesday evening Jill arrived at the Taylors' house with the invitations. Val and Jill's friend Alison had designed a flyer, and Jill's father had photocopied it at his office. Alison had drawn a border of happy animals and smiling people that surrounded the basic party information — time, place, and date. Erin and Teddy helped stuff and stamp the envelopes, and Doc mailed them the next morning on his way to Animal Inn.

That week the construction workers finally completed the new wing, and the painters took over. Luckily they didn't make much noise, to Pat Dempwolf's relief. By the time they'd finish, the new cages Doc had ordered were due to arrive, as well as the other equipment for the treatment room and the infirmary. Everything was proceeding according to schedule.

Val was so busy that she didn't have much time to spend with Donna, but whenever she had a free moment, she dropped into the grooming salon. What she saw fascinated her. Donna knew exactly what she was doing, and every animal she cared for came out looking absolutely beautiful. Val was particularly interested in the artistic way Donna clipped the poodles and schnauzers — Val had some experience with shaving certain areas of her father's patients before surgery, but that was something else entirely. Because she wanted to learn everything she could about all aspects of animal care, Val asked Donna if she could borrow some of her books on grooming, and Donna readily agreed.

"What are you reading, Vallie?" Erin asked one night. Val had finished her homework and her chores and was curled up on the living room sofa studying one of Donna's books.

"*Creative Poodle Clipping,*" Val told her. "It's very interesting. I didn't know there were so many different hairstyles for dogs — there's the pet clip for puppies and poodles that aren't entered in shows, and the Continental and the English Saddle and dozens more. Look at this one." She showed Erin a photograph of a red toy poodle with a fan-shaped pouf of hair on top of its head. "He's a champion — Glendora's Marmaduke Royal Red."

"Oh, he's so cute!" Erin cooed. Then she giggled. "His name's longer than he is!"

"Will you guys *please* pipe down?" Teddy said. He was lying on the floor, watching his favorite television show. "The alien's gonna zap the humanoid!"

"Can Donna do all that?" Erin asked.

Val nodded. "She sure can. Mrs. Blackman brought in her standard poodle yesterday, and when the dog left, she looked just like this one here." She showed Erin another picture.

"They're all so beautiful," Erin sighed. "They look like ballerinas with their slender, delicate legs and their hair all fluffy, kind of like tutus, only on the wrong end. Are you going to learn how to clip poodles like this, Vallie?"

Val shrugged. "Maybe. It might be kind of fun."

"Can I learn, too?" Erin asked eagerly. "Can I come out to Animal Inn after school one day and watch Donna? Maybe she'd let me help her do things like combing and brushing and painting the dogs' toenails. Look at this one, Vallie — the white poodle with the purple ribbons in its hair. It has purple toenails to match!" She gazed thoughtfully down at Jocko and Sunshine, who were stretched out on either side of Teddy. "I could practice on our dogs. Bright red toenails for Jocko to go with his red collar, and pink polish for Sunshine — or maybe green. Will you ask Donna for some nail polish tomorrow?"

"I'll think about it," Val promised. She was glad to see Erin showing some interest in Animal Inn. Sometimes she felt that her little sister spent too much time practicing her ballet in the basement, at the *barre* Doc had installed many years ago for their mother. If Erin started coming to Animal Inn, maybe she'd learn to love animals as much as Val and Doc did. Well, maybe not quite as much — nobody, not even Doc, was as much of an animal nut as Val.

Donna was grateful for Val's suggestion that Erin lend her a hand one or two days a week after school.

"To tell you the truth, Vallie, I've been getting pretty tired lately," she confessed. "Dr. Moss says it's because of the baby, and I'm not supposed to overdo things. Tell Erin to come in whenever she feels like it."

The very next day Erin biked to Animal Inn right after school. Val didn't see her at all until five o'clock, when both the clinic and the grooming salon had closed. Then Erin came in, wreathed in smiles. "I had so much fun!" she told Val and Toby. "I didn't really do much, but I watched Donna and handed her things when she asked for them. And she let me help her shampoo the cutest little dog. It was covered with long white hair. I think she said it was a *lahsapso.*"

Val grinned. "A Lhasa apso," she corrected. "That had to be Prince William Gerhart. He's the only one in town."

"Well, you should have seen him when we were through. His coat was as soft and smooth as silk, and Donna let me tie a little blue bow on his head to keep the hair out of his eyes!"

Toby groaned faintly, but Erin paid no attention. "I'm coming out again on Saturday right after my ballet class," she went on. "Donna says she can really use my help then. She has lots of appointments. No poodles, though — she says all the poodle people and a lot of others, too, are waiting till right before the Humane Society Dog Show to have their pets groomed. But on Saturday, she's gong to clip an Airedale, and I'm going to watch!"

Mike had come into the waiting room in time to hear what Erin was saying, and now he said, "Well, well, if it ain't my old pal Erin! Long time no see, stranger. You gonna start workin' here like your big sister? Don't tell me there's gonna be *three* vets in the Taylor family."

"Oh, Mike," Erin laughed, "I'm not going to become a vet. I still want to be a ballet dancer like Mommy." She wrinkled her nose. "I don't really like being around sick animals, but the animals Donna takes care of aren't sick. You're going to be seeing a lot of me from now on."

"That's fine by me," Mike said. "And it ain't a bad idea to add another string to your bow — if the ballet business don't pan out, you can always get a job at some pet primpin' parlor." He turned to Val. "Vallie, you know where Doc is? I been lookin' for him to give me my orders for the night, but I ain't seen him around."

"Dad had to go to Mr. Stambaugh's farm to vaccinate his turkey chicks," Val said. "He left a list for you on the reception desk."

"Guess I'll be on my way," Toby said, but before he could leave Val suggested, "Why don't you stick around for a while? Erin and I don't have to be home till six, and I thought maybe the three of us could take turns riding The Ghost out in the back pasture. He gets lonely all by himself when we don't have a horse patient to keep him company."

That plan sounded good to Toby, so he, Val, and Erin said good-bye to Mike and went outside. Val and Toby each took turns riding the big dapple-gray gelding around the pasture for a while, but Erin preferred to watch because her ballet teacher said that horseback riding was bad for a ballet dancer's leg muscles. She and Val sat on the top rail of the fence watching Toby and The Ghost amble along the little stream that ran through the pasture. Erin said, "It's funny about animals, isn't it, Vallie?"

"What's funny?"

"Well, they come in so many different sizes. I mean, Prince William isn't much bigger than a cat, and The Ghost is as big as a car. Wouldn't it be weird if people were like that? And then there's their fur. Poodles have all those curls, but horses are smooth and shiny. If you don't clip poodles regularly, their fur gets long and curly all over, but horses' hair just stays short. I wonder why that is."

"I wonder, too. I asked Dad about it once, but he didn't know either," Val said. "And if Dad doesn't know, I guess nobody does."

The sisters sat in comfortable silence, enjoying the warmth of the late afternoon sunshine and the sweet scent of freshly cut grass.

"I wonder if Daddy would let me have a poodle," Erin mused aloud. "Just a little one — like Lila Bascombe's, or like that toy poodle with the fancy topknot in Donna's book. I'd want it to be a girl, and I'd call it Pavlova. She was a very famous ballet dancer."

Val sighed. "Erin, we already have two perfectly good dogs and Cleveland and the chickens, the rabbits, and the duck, not to mention Dandy, your very own canary, and Teddy's hamsters.''

"I know, but Dandy's the only one of our pets who's really mine. I'd like a little poodle to play with and wash and groom and clip. . . .''

Val poked her playfully in the arm. "You've got poodles on the brain! And if you're so eager to practice dog grooming, start with Jocko and Sunshine. They haven't had baths in ages.''

"It's not the same thing," Erin said wistfully.

"Well, when you're a famous ballerina, you can have as many poodles as you like in that Park Avenue penthouse you say you're going to live in. But right now you're stuck with Jocko and Sunshine.'' Val jumped to the ground. "Hey, Toby, it's my turn,'' she called, and Toby turned the horse in her direction, urging him into a jog-trot.

As Val watched them approach, her heart swelled with love for The Ghost. Of all the animals in the world, she loved horses best, and of all the horses in the world, she was sure there was none to compare with her very own Ghost. Somehow she just couldn't imagine feeling the same way about a yappy little poodle, no matter how cute and cuddly it was.

After Toby turned The Ghost over to Val, she

looked over at the small animal clinic with its brand-new extension, built of the same rosy brick as the older structure. "Just think, Ghost!" she said happily. "The big party's only two weeks away, and then the boarding kennel will be open for business. It's going to be a wonderful party, and you're invited. I hope you won't mind being the only horse there. . . ."

"Vallie, Toby's going home, and I think we'd better leave, too," Erin called to her from her perch on top of the fence. "It's a quarter to six."

"Coming," Val shouted, waving at her sister. She nudged The Ghost with her heels, and he broke into his comfortable rocking-chair canter for one last circuit of the pasture.

Chapter
7

The next week was a busy one at Animal Inn, made even busier for Val because Toby called in sick on Tuesday. He had a virus and he sounded awful, but he hoped to be back in school and at work by Thursday. That meant that Val had to do double duty, relieving Pat at the reception desk and helping Doc with his patients, as well as making sure that the animals in the infirmary and in the large animal clinic got the proper medications and were fed on schedule.

Doc was trying to be in two — sometimes even three places at once. He was dashing between patients to consult with the workers who were laying the tile floor in the new wing, fixing a leaky faucet in Donna's grooming salon, and checking out the shipment of new cages that arrived late Wednesday afternoon. To his dismay, they were not the ones he had ordered, so he refused to accept them.

"Gee, Dad," Val said worriedly as the huge

67

truck lumbered out of the parking lot. "Do you think they'll send us the right ones in time? We have so many reservations for the week after the party — if we don't have any place to put them, what are we going to do?"

"Pat's calling the company now," Doc told her with a sigh. "Apparently there was a mix-up. Those cages were supposed to go to a veterinary clinic in Maryland, so I can only assume that the Maryland clinic got ours. Everything will be straightened out in a few days — I hope!"

"I hope so, too." Val followed her father back into Animal Inn, where they were greeted by several impatient pet owners.

"Say, Doc, I've been waiting for more than half an hour for you to take a look at Wilbur's sore foot," a red-faced man complained, and his sad-eyed springer spaniel lifted a furry paw and whined.

"Now, Jeremiah Stambaugh, I've been waiting a lot longer than you," said the plump, middle-aged woman in a flowered housedress, who was holding a thin black-and-white cat on her lap. "And Blackie's in a lot worse shape than your old hound!"

"Wilbur isn't a hound," Mr. Stambaugh snapped. "He's the best hunting dog a man ever had, and don't you forget it!"

Val quickly picked Blackie up, scratching the

cat under its chin. "Blackie's first, Mr. Stambaugh," she said. "Dad will take care of him right away, and then it's Wilbur's turn. We're kind of short-handed today, so we're running a little late."

"Oh, Doc," Pat sang out from behind the reception desk, "I talked to those cage people, and the ones you ordered will be here a week from today. And a Mr. Brown wants you to make a house call today when you have a chance. His pet, Rocky, has a bad cold, but he says he can't bring him in."

Following Val and Blackie to the treatment room, Doc paused. "Rocky? I don't think I know him — or Mr. Brown, either. What *is* Rocky?"

Pat shrugged, reaching for the ringing phone. "Search me. The man just said Rocky had a real stuffy nose, and he couldn't breathe. I wrote down the address right here — " She picked up the phone. "Good afternoon, Animal Inn. May I help you?"

As soon as office hours were over, Doc and Val got into the van and headed for Mr. Brown's house and the mysterious Rocky. Mr. Brown was a young man who had just moved to Essex with his wife and their pet, Rocky. Rocky turned out to be a ten-foot-long python in a glass-enclosed case that was as big as a small room, with a large, gnarled branch running from top to bottom. He was wrapped around the branch, all ten feet of him, but he didn't look happy.

"Wow! That's some snake!" Val exclaimed, widening her hazel eyes. "He's beautiful!"

"He is, isn't he?" Mrs. Brown said. She was a tall, slim young woman wearing tight jeans and a sleeveless T-shirt. Val thought she was very pretty. "Rocky's had colds before, but they've never been as bad as this. We were going to give him to some friends of ours who live in Florida so they could set him free in the Everglades. And then he got sick." She turned to Doc. "Do you know what to do for him?"

Doc set down his black bag. "To tell you the truth, Mrs. Brown, I haven't had many pythons as patients. But I think I can help." He rolled up his sleeves. "Vallie, do you want to help me with this?"

"Sure!" Val smiled at Mr. and Mrs. Brown. "I'm going to be a vet like my father, and he's taught me everything he knows. I may not be very old, but I've had a terrific teacher!"

Mr. Brown, who was not much bigger around than Rocky, nodded. "A lot of people don't understand about snakes. They're real good pets."

Following Doc's instructions, Mr. Brown gently detached Rocky from the tree trunk and carried the first few feet of him into the bathroom, while Doc took the middle and Val brought up the rear. Then Doc turned on the warm water in the sink, telling Mr. Brown to hold Rocky's head under it. Rocky didn't seem to mind, and by the time they were through, he was looking much more wide awake.

"The warmth and the moisture allow him to breathe easier," Doc said to Mr. Brown. "If you and your wife can manage this treatment several times a day, it will do him a lot of good."

They put Rocky back into his glass house, and Doc gave the Browns some antibiotics to dissolve in water which they were to give him at regular intervals so he wouldn't develop pneumonia. When Doc and Val left, Rocky's eyes were wide open, and his little forked tongue was darting in and out of his mouth in a much more healthy fashion.

"It would be nice," Doc murmured as he drove away, "if people mentioned what sort of pet they have when they ask me to make a house call. Good thing I just read an article on pythons the other day in one of my medical journals."

"You were fantastic, Dad," Val said.

Doc glanced at her and smiled. "So were you, honey. But you may *not* invite Rocky to the party!"

Val giggled. "I thought maybe you were going to say that!"

* * *

71

It was almost seven o'clock by the time Val and Doc got home. Mrs. Racer had already left, but the tempting aroma of whatever she had cooked for supper still lingered in the air. Val was about to check the oven to see what it was, when Teddy dashed into the hall, hollering, "*Dad!* You gotta talk to Erin, and then I'm gonna *kill* her!"

"That sounds a little drastic." Doc bent down to give Teddy a hug and a kiss. "What's the problem?"

"Jocko, that's what!" Teddy said. "He's *bald*!"

"Oh, Teddy, he is not." Erin came out of the living room and stood on tiptoe to kiss Doc on the cheek. "Hi, Daddy. Hi, Vallie. You're awfully late — Teddy and I already ate, but there's plenty left."

"He is too bald!" Teddy scowled at her from under the visor of the Phillies baseball cap he always wore. "He doesn't have any fur on his rear end!"

Puzzled, Doc said, "He doesn't? How did that happen?"

Val had a very strong feeling that she knew, particularly since Erin was wearing one of Doc's old shirts over her leotard and tights, like the smock Donna always wore when she worked.

"Erin, you didn't borrow Donna's clippers, did you?" she asked.

"No," Erin said brightly. "I'm not ready for that

yet. I'm still learning. But I'll never get good at clipping if I don't practice, so I used Daddy's scissors, the ones he trims his beard with, to practice on Jocko. I gave him a shampoo. I'm sure he'll feel much cooler without all that extra fur. He's not bald at all — Teddy's exaggerating.''

"I am *not* 'zaggerating!" Teddy yelled. "Wait till you see him, Dad. He looks rickulous!"

"Ridiculous," Doc corrected automatically.

"That's what I said." Teddy trotted into the living room, followed by Val, Erin, and Doc. "Jocko?" he called. "Where are you, boy? Come on out — it's okay. We won't laugh at you, honest."

But there was no sign of the little black-and-white dog, or of Sunshine, either. Cleveland, who was washing himself in Doc's favorite armchair by the fireplace, was the only animal in sight.

A sad little whine from the dining room led Val to investigate. She found Sunshine lying down beside the table and peering beneath it. He wagged his tail when he saw Val, but he didn't move. Val dropped down on all fours beside him and found herself face to muzzle with Jocko. Very gently she took his front paws and pulled him out of his hiding place. The front half of him looked perfectly normal, but from his rib cage to his tail was a different story. All his shaggy black-and-white fur had been cut very short, as though he had had a close encounter with a small lawnmower. He whined again and tucked his tail between his hind legs. Sunshine whined in sympathy with his friend.

"See?" Teddy cried. "What did I tell you?"

"Oh, gosh," Val breathed.

"I know it's not very smooth, the way Donna does it, but I was only using scissors," Erin mumbled, twisting the tails of Doc's shirt into a knot. "His fur will grow back, won't it?" she asked her father nervously. "I didn't hurt him or anything. And he *will* be lots cooler, now that it's getting so hot. . . ."

"Erin, I don't think this was a very good idea," Doc said. He stroked his beard, but Val thought he kept his hand over his mouth longer than was really necessary — perhaps to conceal a smile? Jocko did look pretty silly! "I don't think Jocko likes it very much. He's not a poodle, you know. Poodles are used to this sort of thing, and Jocko's not." He put his arm around Erin. "Honey, what's done is done, but don't do it again, okay? No more experimenting with our pets. I'm glad that you're helping Donna and learning to do what she does. But do *not* practice on Sunshine or Cleveland! Get the picture?"

Erin buried her face in his chest. "Okay. I'm sorry, Daddy. I didn't mean to make Jocko unhappy.

I just thought he'd look so cute with a Continental clip. . . ."

"If you think I'm going to walk Jocko tonight when he looks like that and let everybody laugh at him, you got another think coming!" Teddy blustered.

"Erin will be in charge of walking Jocko until his fur grows back," Doc said firmly. "And if people laugh, she can explain to them why he looks that way. Have you fed your chickens, Teddy?"

"Uh . . . no," Teddy mumbled.

"Well then, I suggest you do it right now while Erin walks the dogs."

"I'll feed Cleveland and the rabbits and the duck," Val said quickly. "And then you and I can eat, Dad."

"Raaoow!" said Cleveland, winding around Val's ankles and trying to look like a starving cat.

"There's pot roast for you, Daddy, and a vegetable casserole for Vallie," Erin said as she fastened the leashes to Jocko's and Sunshine's collars.

"Why were you so late?" Teddy asked after he had done his chores and Val and Doc were seated at the butcher-block table in the kitchen.

"We had a house call," Val told him, putting

some salad onto Doc's plate. "A ten-foot python with a stuffy nose."

Teddy's eyes widened. "A python? Wow, that's neat! Are you going to see him again? Can I come, too? What's his name? How did he get a cold? I didn't know snakes could catch cold."

"If it has a nose it can catch a cold," Doc said. "The python's name is Rocky, and if we have to pay another call on him, maybe you can come along. But right now, don't you have some homework to do?"

"Well, yeah, kind of. . . ."

"Then you'd better do it. And *not* in front of the television. Now, scoot!" Doc gave a playful tug to the visor of Teddy's cap.

"Okay. Boy, a ten-foot-long python! Wait'll I tell the gang!"

Teddy ran out of the kitchen, scooping up a handful of Mrs. Racer's oatmeal-raisin cookies on the way. He passed Erin, who had just come back from walking the dogs.

"Nobody laughed at Jocko at all, so there!" she said with her nose in the air.

"They will tomorrow!" Teddy shouted as he pounded up the stairs.

* * *

It was nine o'clock, and Val had come into her sister's room to say good night. Erin, in a ruffled cotton nightgown, was sitting up in her bed with one of Donna's grooming books on her lap instead of a book about ballet, which she usually read. Her canary's cage was covered for the night, but Dandy chirped sleepily when he heard Val's voice.

Yawning, Erin closed the book, putting it on the bedside table and snuggling down under the covers. "I did all my homework," she said. Then, in a small voice, "Vallie, is Daddy really mad at me because of what I did to Jocko? I'd hate it if he was."

Val sat down on the bed. "No, silly, of course not. He's coming in to kiss you good night in a few minutes. But you have to admit it was a pretty dumb thing to do. There's no way you're going to turn Jocko into a poodle, no matter how hard you try!"

Erin sighed. "I know. Only I needed the practice, and Jocko just happened to be there. If I'd had Donna's electric clippers, he would have looked much better. The next time — "

"There's not going to *be* a next time," Val said sternly. "You promised, remember?"

"Yes, I remember. But Donna's teaching me how to use the clippers, and I've been reading a lot about it. Did you know that those electric clippers have a built-in safety factor so you can't possibly cut a dog's skin?''

"Good." Val reached over and turned out the light on Erin's bedside table. "Now good night, sleep tight. . . ."

" . . . Don't let the bedbugs bite," Erin murmured. "Vallie?"

"What?"

"Are you *absolutely* sure Daddy's not mad?"

Val stroked her sister's silky blonde hair. "I am absolutely, positively sure," she said softly.

"Okay." Erin rolled over and burrowed her head into the pillow. " 'Night, Vallie.''

" 'Night, Erin.''

Chapter
8

On Sunday Doc drove Val and Erin to The Party Palace at the shopping mall, where they bought rainbow-striped tablecloths and napkins, plates, cups, and plenty of plastic knives, forks, and spoons.

"Daddy, could we get some balloons and paper streamers, too?" Erin asked. "We could decorate the new wing inside and out, so it would look really special."

"Sure, honey — why not?" Doc said, and Erin happily began adding streamers and balloons to their basket.

"Dad, I just had an awful thought," Val said. "What if it rains? We're planning on having the celebration outside, but if it rains what are we going to do?"

Doc shrugged. "Move the party indoors, I guess. But according to the long-range weather forecast, Saturday's supposed to be sunny and hot."

"I sure hope so! It's going to be terribly crowded

if everybody has to stay inside. I think everyone we invited is going to come, and most of them are bringing their pets. Guess we'd better just keep our fingers crossed."

"I might find it difficult to treat my patients that way," Doc said solemnly, and Val laughed.

"Okay — Erin and I will keep *our* fingers crossed then!"

The following Tuesday the cages Doc had ordered were finally delivered, and the work crew began to install them. The painting was finished, and the floors had been laid. The equipment for the second treatment room, the expanded infirmary, and the new isolation ward arrived on Wednesday, and Toby, who was fully recovered from his virus, spent most of his time helping Mike Strickler put everything in place. Mike was glad for the extra work — he never seemed to get tired, and his corny jokes kept Toby laughing.

When Val got to Animal Inn each day after school, she assisted her father with his patients. As Mike had predicted, there were a lot of them. Many of Donna's clients who used to go to Dr. Callahan in Harrisburg now realized that there was a better, less expensive vet much closer to home. Val wasn't surprised at all by the new patients, because she'd always known her dad was the best.

Since this was the week before the Humane Society's dog show, Donna's grooming service was very much in demand. Erin came out every day that she didn't have ballet class to help Donna prepare all the dogs for the show. She loved every minute of it and was proud that Donna was giving her more and more responsibility.

But on Thursday Erin dashed into the waiting room, where Val was covering the reception desk for Pat, who was taking a coffee break.

"Vallie, we've got a problem," she whispered into Val's ear.

"What kind of problem?" Val asked as she entered another reservation for the boarding kennel into Doc's red book.

"A *big* one! Donna had an appointment with her baby doctor — "

"Her obstetrician?"

"That's right. It was for three o'clock, because she didn't have any dogs to groom until four. But Mrs. Bascombe just came in with Marie Antoinette for a shampoo and a clip, and she says she had an appointment with Donna for three-thirty, but Marie Antoinette's not in Donna's book. I guess maybe Pat forgot to write it down or something. Anyway, Mrs. Bascombe and Lila are coming back at four-thirty to pick up Marie Antoinette, and it's four o'clock now and — "

"Whoa, slow down, Erin," Val interrupted. "When will Donna be back?"

Erin gasped for breath. "Donna just called to say the doctor was late because he was delivering a baby, and she won't be back till five, and what am I going to do?" Erin was clearly very upset. "Her four o'clock appointment canceled at the last minute, so the only one to worry about is Marie Antoinette."

Just then Pat returned from her coffee break.

"Uh . . . Pat, do you happen to remember making ·an appointment for Donna to groom Marie Antoinette Bascombe this afternoon?" Val asked casually.

Pat smiled. "Why, I sure do. Three-thirty, it was. I wrote it down the way I always do."

"It's not in Donna's book," Erin said. "I looked three times, honest I did. Marie Antoinette's here, but Donna isn't."

Pat's smile faded. "Oh, dear! I know I wrote it down, I just know I did. . . . Oh, dear," she said again. "What with all the phone calls we've been getting, maybe I put it in the wrong book!" She opened Doc's blue appointment book and ran her plump finger down that day's page. Her face fell. "Oh, dear. I did! Wasn't that silly of me? Is Mrs. Bascombe very upset?"

"Not yet," Erin said.

"That's okay, Pat," Val put in quickly. "Don't worry about it."

As Toby came into the waiting room, Val grabbed his arm.

"Toby, we need you," she said. "You have to help me give Marie Antoinette a bath!"

Toby stared at her. "Marie Antoinette? Wasn't she that French queen who got her head chopped off?"

"Not *that* Marie Antoinette! This one's an apricot miniature poodle who's waiting for a shampoo and a clip, but Donna's not here," Val told him.

"No way!" Toby scowled at both Val and Erin. "No way, no how! Nosirree!"

A few minutes later, Val and Toby were kneeling beside a tub in the grooming salon, up to their elbows in suds. Marie Antoinette, her red-gold curls sopping wet, was whimpering loudly and trying to escape.

"I can't *believe* this," Toby muttered, grabbing the little dog and pulling her back into the tub. "I said I wasn't ever going to mess around with the beauty parlor, and here I am, washing this dopey poodle! I oughta have my head examined!"

"*Wowowowowow!*" wailed Marie Antoinette.

"She doesn't like it any more than you do," Val told him. "So you're even. And I promise I won't tell a soul." She scratched the poodle gently under her chin and crooned. "There, there, Toni. You're going to be just fine. A clean animal is a healthy animal, and you don't want to be an *un*healthy animal, do you?"

"Toni?" Toby repeated. "I thought this pooch's name was Marie Antoinette."

"Well, it is, but that's what Lila calls her when she talks about her, and she talks about her all the time," Val said. Mimicking Lila, she chirped, "Toni has a pedigree that goes back *hundreds* of years. Toni cost *hundreds* of dollars. Toni's won *hundreds* of prizes."

"Gimme a break!" Toby sighed. "Now I guess we have to rinse her, right?"

"*Hundreds* of times," Val said, grinning as she picked up the little poodle and plopped her into a second tub.

By the time Marie Antoinette had been washed, rinsed, and dried, there was still no sign of Donna.

"I'm outa here," Toby said, heading for the door. "Mike needs me — and if he doesn't, Doc does. You're on your own."

84

"Thanks, Toby," Val said, trying to detach the little dog from the laces of her sneakers. Marie Antoinette was chewing on them happily, growling and yipping.

Erin popped her head in the doorway. "Vallie, Mrs. Bascombe and Lila are going to be here any minute! They're going to be furious when they find out that she hasn't been clipped. Mrs. Bascombe told me that they expect her to win Best in Show at the dog show on Sunday."

Val looked at her watch. It was twenty after four.

"I think I'd better talk to Dad," she said. She picked up the poodle and thrust it into Erin's arms. "Keep an eye on her — and watch out for your sneakers! I'll be back in a flash!"

But she wasn't back in a flash. When she burst into the treatment room, Doc said, "Vallie, where have you been? Jack Botterbusch just brought in his dog, O'Reilly. O'Reilly had a fight with a stray cat, and his ears are badly scratched. Give me a hand, will you?"

O'Reilly, a scrawny mixed breed, wasn't the easiest patient Val had ever handled, and by the time she and Doc had tended to his wounds, it was a quarter to five. As soon as the bandaged dog was returned to his anxious owner, Val told her father

85

about Marie Antoinette and the Bascombes.

"Toby and I gave Toni a shampoo," she said, "but Mrs. Bascombe and Lila will have a fit because Donna hasn't clipped her."

"I'll explain the situation," Doc assured her. "Just give me a few minutes to wash up — I don't want to go in there all covered with O'Reilly's blood."

Val hurried back to the grooming salon, where she discovered Lila and her mother. They were having a fit.

"*Look* at that dog!" Mrs. Bascombe shrieked the minute she saw Val. "She's ruined, absolutely *ruined*!"

"Poor, *poor* Toni!" Lila wailed melodramatically. "What have they *done* to you?"

Val stared at the little dog, and Marie Antoinette stared back. If it was possible for a dog to look sheepish, this one did, Val thought. And no wonder — her hindquarters were clipped smooth as silk, but the fluffy ruff that should have surrounded her shoulders like a feather boa was nothing more than a scraggy circle of fur.

Going over to her sister, who was wearing one of Donna's smocks, her face paper-white, Val whispered, "Erin, You *didn't*!"

"I just wanted to help," Erin murmured. Her eyes were brimming with tears. "I was afraid they'd be mad at Donna if Marie Antoinette wasn't ready. Everything was all right until I started to trim the fur on her shoulders. And then it wasn't even, so I had to trim a little more off one side, but that made the other side too long, so — "

"I get the picture," Val sighed.

"This is an outrage!" Mrs. Bascombe blustered. "Nothing like this ever happened at The Pink Poodle! Obviously Ida Potter was the one who knew what she was doing." She glared at Erin and Val. "I demand to speak to your father! He must fire Donna Hartman immediately!"

"He'll be here in a minute," Val said shakily. "But Mrs. Bascombe, it wasn't Donna's fault. I understand that you're distressed, but — "

"So am I," Lila said, scowling. "After all, Toni is *my* dog."

Trembling, Erin stepped forward. "Mrs. Bascombe, I . . ." She swallowed hard. "I . . ."

Val made her decision on the spot. Before Erin could get another word out, she said loudly, "Donna didn't clip Marie Antoinette. I did."

Three pairs of eyes (four, counting the poodle's) focused on her.

Almost in one voice, Lila and her mother squawked, "*You* did?"

"That's right." Val shook off Erin's restraining hand. "Donna had a doctor's appointment, so she couldn't do it. I've been reading a lot about poodle grooming, and I thought I could handle it." She looked at the little dog, who was now wrapped in Lila's arms. "Guess I was wrong. Sorry, Toni."

Lila wasn't too distressed to smile nastily at her. Val knew exactly what she was thinking — for once Val was in trouble instead of Lila, and she was enjoying every second of it.

Mrs. Bascombe wasn't enjoying anything at all. She was angrier than ever. Even her carefully styled hair seemed to bristle with rage. "*Well!*" she gasped. "Well, I never!"

Before she could say anything else Doc came into the room.

"Doctor Taylor," Mrs. Bascombe snapped, turning to him, "do you mean to tell me that you allow a mere *child* to be responsible for grooming a valuable animal like Marie Antoinette?"

"She cost *hundreds* of dollars," Lila added.

"I know," Val said through gritted teeth.

"But Mrs. Bascombe, it wasn't — " Erin began.

Doc took in the situation at a glance. Replying

to Mrs. Bascombe, he said, "No, I most certainly do not. If you'll excuse me, I'd like to speak to my daughters for a moment."

"Speak to them all you like," Mrs. Bascombe said. "But nothing you can say will alter the fact that due to your negligence, my dog — "

"*My* dog," Lila whined.

" — Lila's dog will be unable to compete in the Humane Society show on Sunday, or indeed in any other show for months to come! Negligence, that's what it is! Sheer negligence!" She turned on her heel and headed for the door. "Come, Lila," she barked. "We're going straight to your father's office. As for you, Doctor Taylor, you'll be hearing from our lawyer first thing tomorrow morning!"

" 'Bye, Val," Lila said sweetly. "See you in school tomorrow — if you dare show up!"

The door slammed behind them, and Erin sank into a chair, sobbing. "Oh, Daddy, I'm so sorry! Vallie told them she clipped Marie Antoinette, but she didn't. It was me!"

"I figured that out." Doc's usually smiling face was grim.

"Dad, are they going to sue us?" Val asked anxiously.

"So it appears." Shaking his head, Doc looked

down at Erin. "Erin, whatever possessed you? You promised not to do any more experimenting — and please don't tell me that promise only applied to our pets. I never thought I'd say this, but I'm very disappointed in you."

"I was — only — trying to — help," Erin gasped between sobs.

Val sat on the arm of Erin's chair, putting an arm around her sister. "She was, Dad. You know how Erin hates it when people get mad at each other. She didn't want the Bascombes to be angry at Donna, and I wanted to help *her*, so I said I'd done it." She sighed. "Only none of it helped anybody at all." Scowling, she added, "Now I see why Lila's so mean — she takes after her mother! What does Mrs. Bascombe want to sue you for? Why doesn't she sue *me*? She thinks I'm to blame."

The phone rang and Val answered it. She heard Donna's cheerful voice saying, "Vallie, is that you? Would you believe I just saw the doctor? No sense in my coming to Animal Inn now, since it's so late. Please tell your dad I'll be in bright and early tomorrow morning. Good thing I only had one appointment this afternoon. Did Erin reschedule Lester Shugart's cocker spaniel?"

"He canceled," Val mumbled.

"Isn't that a blessing! Then I suppose everything's been nice and quiet over there."

"Well . . ." Val mumbled, but then decided not to say anything.

"You sound a bit tired. I hope it's quitting time for you," Donna said, a bit concerned. "Oh, Val, tell Erin I bought her a little present. I tell you, Vallie, I don't know what I'd do without her. She's a wonderful help to me! Tell her I said that, won't you?"

Val sighed. "Yes, Donna. I'll tell her."

Chapter 9

Nobody said much of anything on the ride back home. Erin sat in the back with her and Val's bicycles, sniffling every now and then, and Val sat next to Doc in the passenger seat, lost in gloomy thought. When Doc drove the van into the driveway, Val and Erin took out the bicycles, then plodded silently up the path to the front door. Erin immediately ran inside and up the stairs, shutting the door of her room behind her.

Mrs. Racer came out of the kitchen, smiling. "On time for once!" she said. "There's a little roast beef in the oven for you and Erin, Doc, and a vegetable casserole for you, Vallie — it's a nice recipe I cut out of the Sunday paper. My stars!" She peered at their glum faces. "You look like you lost your last friend. Did a patient go and die on you?" She knew that both Doc and Val were always very sad when they couldn't save one of their animal patients. "And where's Erin?"

Absently patting Jocko and Sunshine, who were welcoming him home with their usual excited jumps and yips, Doc put down his medical bag. "Erin went upstairs to her room. And no, Mrs. Racer, we didn't lose a patient. We're just. . . ."

"Tired," Val said as she picked up Cleveland and snuggled him. "We're really tired. Where's Teddy?"

"He's eating over at Billy's. I gave him permission." She looked anxiously at Doc. "That's all right, isn't it? He'll be home by seven-thirty. Maybe I should have called you, but. . . ."

Doc forced a smile. "Yes, it's all right."

A horn honked outside, and Mrs. Racer took off her apron and handed it to Val. "That's m'son Henry. You sure there's nothing wrong?"

Val smiled, too. "Absolutely sure. 'Night, Mrs. Racer. See you tomorrow."

The old woman nodded, but she looked worried as she trotted out the door.

Putting Cleveland down, Val trudged into the kitchen. As usual, everything smelled wonderful, but she didn't have any appetite. Neither did Doc. They served themselves and then sat at the butcher-block table in silence, picking at their food.

Finally Val said, "Dad, what happens when somebody sues somebody?"

Doc shrugged. "A couple of lawyers get very rich. And sometimes small business people get very poor."

"Small business people like you." Val poked at her casserole with her fork. Then she glanced over at the counter. She saw lots of tins that she knew were filled with the cookies Mrs. Racer had baked for the party. But Val was definitely not in a party mood.

Doc pushed back his plate, which was still filled with tender roast beef, asparagus, and scalloped potatoes. "Vallie, why don't you take some supper up to Erin? I'm going to make a phone call."

"To your lawyer?" Val asked.

"No — to the Bascombes." Doc picked up the Essex phone book and began looking under the B's.

Val's eyes widened. "The Bascombes?"

"Yes. I've served on various committees with Tom Bascombe in recent years and he's not a bad sort, though his wife *can* be a pain. Still, I'm going to ask them if we can get together and discuss this thing before the lawyers start working." He reached for the phone and dialed. A moment later, Val heard him say, "Tom? Ted Taylor here. . . . Yes, I know she's upset. So am I. I was wondering if we could all talk about the situation tonight. . . . Yes, tonight . . . . No, it *can't* wait until the morning. . . .

94

About half an hour at your place? Good. I'll be there.''

As soon as he hung up, Val said, "Dad, can I come, too?''

Doc shook his head. "Honey, this isn't your fight. I understand your trying to protect Erin, but Mrs. Bascombe was right — Donna's grooming operation is part of Animal Inn, and that makes me responsible if anything goes wrong.''

Val planted her hands on her hips. "As far as the Bascombes are concerned, I'm the bad guy, so I ought to be there.''

"No, Vallie.'' Erin was standing in the kitchen doorway, her eyes huge in her tear-stained face. "I did it. *I'm* to blame, so I ought to go with Daddy. I have to tell them that it's all my fault.''

Doc stood up and went over to his younger daughter, putting his arm around her. "Erin, somebody has to be here when Teddy gets home, and you're elected. Just don't decide he needs a haircut, okay?''

"Does that mean I can go?'' Val asked.

"Does that mean you're not mad at me anymore?'' Erin asked, clinging to her father.

Doc answered Erin first. "I'm kind of mad,'' he admitted. "I'm mad at what you did, but I understand why you did it.''

Doc held Erin away from him at arm's length. "Erin, what you did was wrong. We all know that. But what's done is done, and you won't do anything like that again, will you." It wasn't a question.

Erin shook her head. "Never! Not ever! The other day, Miss Tamara told me I was the most promising pupil she ever had. I'm going to work extra hard so I can be a ballerina like Mommy was, and you'll be proud of me." A tear trickled down her cheek. "Oh, Daddy, if the Bascombes sue you, will you have to sell Animal Inn? If that happens, I'll just die!"

Val cringed. She couldn't even bear to think about it.

"It won't happen, and you won't die," Doc said firmly. He took a bandana out of the hip pocket of his jeans and held it out to Erin. "Here — blow your nose and dry your eyes. And then I want you to sit down and have some supper. After that you'll walk Jocko and Sunshine and do your homework. When Teddy gets home, tell him that Vallie and I will be back in plenty of time to tuck you both in for the night."

"Then I *can* go!" Val wasn't exactly looking forward to facing Lila and her parents, but she couldn't stand the thought of Doc doing it all by himself. They'd show the Bascombes that the Taylor family stuck together, no matter what!

Doc nodded. "I suggest we make ourselves presentable. I don't know about you, but I definitely need to wash and change — it's been a long, hard day, and I'm feeling kind of grubby."

"Me, too." Val glanced at the kitchen clock. "It's only seven. We have plenty of time — Wyndham Heights is about a ten-minute drive, so we won't be late."

Erin had pulled herself together enough to say good-bye.

"Don't forget to eat," Val reminded her.

"I won't. I'll just heat up Daddy's dinner in the microwave — he hardly touched it," Erin said sadly.

Doc gave her a hug on his way out the door. "Believe me, honey, I won't starve."

Erin tried to smile. "Is that a promise?"

"That's a promise." He kissed the top of her head and started upstairs to change.

"Vallie?" Erin said when he had left the kitchen. "You'll tell those Bascombes that it was me who clipped Marie Antoinette? *Please* say that you will."

Val didn't want to commit herself one way or the other, so she only said, "We'll see." Before her sister could insist that she promise she added, "Hey, Erin, better rescue Dad's plate before Cleveland gobbles up all the asparagus. You know he likes asparagus even more than roast beef!"

It was almost half past seven when Doc stopped the van in front of the Bascombes' colonial style mansion in Wyndham Heights. It was set far back from the street on a velvety green lawn. In the slanting evening sunlight, Val thought the house looked like something out of a movie set, not like a real house where real people lived.

She felt her throat get dry all of a sudden. She really didn't want to face Lila again, and she particularly didn't want to have Mrs. Bascombe yell at her.

"Vallie, you don't have to come in," Doc said gently. "You can just wait here until it's over. This can't be very pleasant for you."

Val smoothed the skirt of the blue chambray dress she'd put on and tucked her thick chestnut hair behind her ears. Raising her chin, she said, "It's not very pleasant for you, either, Dad." Remembering the Winnie-the-Pooh books her mother had read to her when she was very young, she quoted, " 'It isn't much fun for one, but two can stick together, said Pooh.' "

Doc reached out and squeezed her hand. "Okay. Let's do it!"

They got out of the van and marched side by side up the flagstone path to the front door. Doc rang the bell, and almost immediately Mr. Bascombe opened the door. He was a tall man, almost as tall as Doc, but he looked a lot older. His brown hair was thinning, and he'd combed it carefully over the top of his head to cover his bald spot. Mr. Bascombe was wearing a three-piece suit and a tie, as though he were still at his office. Val thought that her father looked much nicer in his slacks, sports shirt, and linen jacket. And Doc had lots of hair, even though it was getting a little gray.

Mr. Bascombe tried to smile. "Good evening, Ted," he said. He peered at Val. "Well, well. I didn't expect to see *you* here. Come in, both of you."

They did. Val and Doc followed Mr. Bascombe into the living room, where they discovered Mrs. Bascombe seated on a brocade-covered sofa, her perfectly manicured hands clasped in her lap. As usual, every hair was in place. As usual, she did not even attempt to smile.

"Have a seat, Ted — and you, too, Valentine." Mr. Bascombe indicated a wing chair and a small settee. After greeting Mrs. Bascombe, Doc took the wing chair and Val perched on the edge of the settee.

Mrs. Bascombe spoke first. "I can't *imagine* why you're here," she said frostily. "I have informed my husband of what happened today at Animal Inn, and I have instructed him to contact our lawyers. I fail to see that we have anything to discuss."

99

"Does Tom feel the same way?" Doc asked.

Mr. Bascombe adjusted the knot of his tie. "Well, Ted, considering the circumstances, it seems to me that Dottie and Lila have a very good reason to — uh — that is to say, considering what Valentine here did to Marie Antoinette. . . ."

Doc stroked his beard. "The fact of the matter, Tom, is that Vallie did absolutely nothing to Lila's dog. It was my younger daughter, Erin, who tried to help Donna Hartman by grooming Marie Antoinette, since Donna was unavailable."

"Donna didn't know that Toni had an appointment today," Val said. "There was a mix-up, because we have two appointment books, and — "

"That," said Mrs. Bascombe, "is *your* problem, not ours. Marie Antoinette was supposed to be cared for by Donna Hartman, *not* by an ignorant child. Whether that child was thirteen or eleven makes absolutely no difference. As I said this afternoon, *you*, Dr. Taylor, are responsible, and we intend to sue Animal Inn and you."

"But that's not fair!" Val cried. "Dad didn't know anything about it! He's the best vet in the world! Ask anybody in Essex!"

Doc smiled at her. "Thanks for the vote of confidence, Vallie." He turned back to Mr. and Mrs. Bascombe. "I fully realize your distress at Marie Antoinette's denuded state, and I agree that as owner and operator of Animal Inn, I must assume full responsibility for whatever happens under the roof of my clinic. However — "

A frantic screech interrupted him from somewhere in the house. *"Daddy! Mummy!* Toni's choking to death! Hurry, she's dying!"

Chapter
10

Val instantly leaped to her feet and dashed off in the direction of Lila's voice. Racing down the hallway, she flung open a door that led to the Bascombes' kitchen. Lila was crouching on the floor next to an overturned garbage container surrounded by scraps of food and holding the little apricot poodle in her arms. Marie Antoinette was gasping and coughing. Lila looked terrified.

"What happened?" Val cried.

"A chicken bone," Lila wailed. "Toni knocked over the garbage and got hold of a chicken bone! She started to chew it up before I could stop her, and I think it's stuck in her throat!"

That was very bad news. Val knew that chicken bones splintered very easiy — if a dog swallowed one, it might pierce the stomach or intestine. And if it got caught in the animal's throat, the dog really could choke to death.

Val knelt down and seized the poodle's jaws,

forcing her mouth open. She shoved her finger and thumb down the dog's throat, trying to reach the bone, but with no success.

"I can't get it out — it's too deep," she muttered.

Doc burst into the kitchen, followed by Mr. and Mrs. Bascombe. One look at the poodle told him all he needed to know. Murmuring soothing words, he too tried to remove the bone, but he couldn't do it, either.

"Give her to me, Lila," he ordered. "I didn't bring my bag with me, so we'll have to take her to Animal Inn. With any luck, I'll be able to use my instruments to get that bone out. If not, I'll have to operate."

"*Operate!*" Lila squawked as Doc took Marie Antoinette from her. "But then she'll have a scar! She'll never win Best in Show if she has a scar!"

"Oh, good grief!" Val shouted, running out the kitchen door after Doc. "It's Toni's *life* that's important, not how she looks or how many prizes she wins!"

When they reached the van, Doc handed the poodle to Val, and they both scrambled inside. Mr. Bascombe had followed them and now he stuck his head in the window next to Val.

"Ted, you do whatever you think is necessary,"

he said. "Valentine is right — the important thing is Toni's life." He reached inside and patted Marie Antoinette. "She's a nice little thing," he said softly.

"We'll give her the best of care," Doc promised.

Mr. Bascombe stepped back as Doc gunned the motor. The van pulled away from the curb and started down the tree-lined street — much too slowly, in Val's opinion.

"Dad, can't we go a little faster?" she asked, holding Marie Antoinette more tightly in her arms. The poodle was quivering, whining, and coughing. What if she died before they got to Animal Inn?

"Not until we reach the main road," Doc said. "Too many children on bikes."

Val knew he was right, of course, but she was glad when they hit Country Club Road and the van picked up speed. "Only a few minutes more, Toni," she said. "Hang in there — don't be scared. Everything's going to be all right." She looked up at Doc. "It *is* going to be all right, isn't it, Dad? Toni's not going to. . . ."

"Die?" Doc finished for her. "No, honey, she's not." He turned onto York Road, driving even faster. "From Toni's symptoms, it appears that a bone fragment has lodged in her esophagus. That's — "

"I know," Val said quickly. "That's the tube

leading from the mouth to the stomach. But if something's stuck there, can't it kill her?"

"Not unless it's big enough to press against the windpipe and prevent her from breathing. Since Toni seems to be breathing all right, that's obviously not the problem. But she's very uncomfortable and very frightened. The best thing you can do for her right now is to try to calm her down."

Val wasn't feeling very calm herself, but she kept her voice low and steady, constantly murmuring to the little dog and patting her reddish-gold fur. Suddenly she remembered something. When she gave pills to Doc's animal patients, particularly big pills, Doc had taught her to stroke the animal's throat downward to help it swallow the medicine. Maybe if she rubbed Toni's throat in the opposite direction, it would help her *un*swallow the bone.

Gently but firmly, Val began to rub the poodle's slender neck upward from her shoulders to her jaw. Toni didn't like that very much — she struggled, coughed, and yipped. And then, as the van sped down Orchard Lane and screeched to a stop in front of Animal Inn, Toni started coughing harder than ever. Her small body twitched and spasmed, and after one last wrenching cough, she lay still.

"Oh, Dad!" Val cried. "I think I've killed her!"

Doc bent over the poodle where she lay in Val's blue chambray-covered lap, and Val squeezed her eyes shut tight as two big tears rolled down her cheeks. "She's dead, isn't she?" she whispered.

"Vallie, open your eyes," Doc said, but Val shook her head violently. She couldn't bear to look.

Then she felt Doc's hand on hers. He lifted it and placed it on Toni's side. To Val's astonishment, she felt movement, warmth, and the frantic beating of the little dog's heart. A moment later, she felt something else — a small, wet tongue licking her hand.

"Toni's not dead. She's perfectly all right. Open your eyes, honey," Doc said again. "I have something to show you."

Val opened one eye, then the other. At first tears misted her vision so she saw nothing but a blur. But when the mist cleared, she saw that Doc was holding something in the palm of his outstretched hand. It was no bigger than a broken matchstick, but Val knew immediately what it was — a tiny piece of chicken bone!

"She coughed it up," Doc told her, grinning.

"Oh, wow!" Val sighed. She slumped down in her seat, weak with relief. Toni, fully recovered now, sat up, shook herself briskly, then planted both front paws on Val's chest and began licking her face. Val hugged her so tight that the little poodle let out a strangled yip.

"Hey, take it easy!" Doc laughed. "Don't break the poor animal's ribs!"

Val buried her face in what was left of Toni's ruff. "I'm just so happy!" she exclaimed. "I was so afraid I'd killed her!" She told Doc about rubbing the poodle's throat. "And when Toni went into convulsions, I was sure that was the end," she finished.

"You did exactly the right thing," Doc said. "I'm proud of you, honey. But I'm not very proud of *me*. I should have thought of it myself."

Val smiled at him. "You had an awful lot on your mind, Dad. You can't think of everything. Besides, two heads are better than one. . . ."

"Especially when one's a cabbage head!" Doc said ruefully. He kissed her cheek. "Thanks, Vallie. You're going to be a fine vet one of these days."

Val beamed with pleasure. Her father's words of praise meant more to her than anything in the world.

"Hey, what's goin' on?" Mike Strickler poked his head in the window of the van, peering at Val, Doc, and Toni. "Saw you drive up here like you were goin' to a fire or something. You got an emergency, Doc?"

"It was, but it's not anymore," Doc told him.

107

Mike looked closely at the poodle. "Ain't that the snooty Bascombes' dog, Marie Anchovy? What's wrong with her? She looks okay to me, except she ain't got much hair."

Val giggled. "Marie *Antoinette*, Mike. She had a chicken bone stuck in her throat, but she just now coughed it up, thank goodness."

"I want to examine her anyway," Doc said, unfastening his seat belt and getting out of the van. "And I'm going to x-ray her to make sure there aren't any more bone fragments in her stomach."

Val unfastened her belt and got out, too, with the poodle in her arms. "I'll bring her into the treatment room, Dad. And then I'm going to call the Bascombes and let them know Toni's all right."

While Mike helped Doc with the examination and X ray, Val dialed the Bascombes' number. She was glad that it was Mr. Bascombe who answered the phone rather than Lila or her mother.

"Mr. Bascombe, it's Val Taylor," she said. "I'm calling from Animal Inn. Toni's okay — we got the bone out, but Dad's giving her a thorough examination now and an X ray to see if she swallowed anything else. Unless he finds something, he won't have to operate."

"Well, I'm very glad to hear it," Mr. Bascombe said. "Thank you for calling, Valentine. And if your father thinks surgery is necessary, please tell him to go ahead — he has my permission."

"I certainly will," Val assured him. "If there's no problem, we'll be bringing Toni home very soon."

She was about to hang up when Mr. Bascombe said, "Uh . . . Valentine, I've persuaded Mrs. Bascombe to change her mind about the suit and we are all extremely grateful to you and your father for taking care of Toni so promptly and efficiently. You can tell your father that, too."

Val smiled. "I sure will! 'Bye, Mr. Bascombe."

As she danced off to tell Doc the good news, Val thought it was a real shame that Lila didn't take after her father. Mr. Thomas Bascombe, she decided, was a very nice man!

Fortunately Doc discovered nothing in Marie Antoinette's stomach that didn't belong there. He and Val returned the poodle to her family, and to Val's surprise, Lila actually thanked them for their efforts. Doc instructed her to feed Toni a soft, bland diet for the next two days, to avoid irritating the dog's tender throat. Mr. Bascombe shook Doc's hand warmly. Then he shook Val's hand, too. Mrs. Bascombe didn't shake their hands, but she nodded in their direction and managed a cold smile.

On her way out the door, Val hesitated and

turned back. "We're having a big party at Animal Inn on Saturday afternoon," she said to Lila and her parents, "to celebrate the opening of our new boarding kennel. It starts at four o'clock, and Dad and I would like all of you to come — Toni, too."

"A party?" Lila's eyes brightened. "Sounds like fun. Can we go, Mummy?"

Mrs. Bascombe sniffed. "You'll have to ask your father. *He's* been making all the decisions around here today."

"Thank you for the invitation, Valentine," Mr. Bascombe said. "We'll certainly try to make it."

As they got back into the van, Val said happily, "Let's hurry home, Dad. I can't wait to tell Erin that she doesn't have to worry anymore — we're not being sued. Now we can all look forward to the party!"

Saturday morning dawned bright and clear — Val knew it did because she was awake to see it. She had set her alarm for five o'clock so she could put the huge turkey in the oven. Erin and Mrs. Racer had glazed and baked two big hams the day before, and Doc and Teddy had made gallons of lemonade. The hams and the lemonade were in the Taylors' old refrigerator in the basement. All the paper goods had been put into the van last night. Val checked and rechecked the list Erin had made. Since there was nothing else for her to do, she showered, put on clean jeans and a brand-new bright red T-shirt, and tied her thick chestnut hair into a ponytail with a matching red ribbon.

At six o'clock she fed Cleveland and the dogs and took Jocko and Sunshine for a long walk.

Six-thirty. It was still too early to wake the rest of the family. Val went out to the backyard and fed her rabbits, Teddy's chickens, and Archie, the duck, telling them all about the party.

"I wish you could come, too," she said, snuggling her favorite rabbit, Flopsy. "But I'll bring you lots of carrots tonight to make up for it. Don't worry, there'll be plenty of corn for you guys," she added to Archie and the chickens.

Finally it was seven o'clock. Unable to wait any longer, Val ran up the stairs and started pounding on doors.

"Come on, sleepyhead," she shouted, sticking her head into Teddy's room. "Time to get up!"

"Rise and shine!" she sang out, opening Erin's door.

Doc opened his door before Val could. "I may not be shining, but I'm up," he said with a yawn. " 'Morning, Vallie."

As he trudged down the hall to the bathroom,

111

Val heard a squawk from Erin's room. *"Vallie!* Cleveland's in my room! Get him out before he scares Dandy to death!"

Val ran to remove Cleveland, almost tripping over Jocko and Sunshine, who were galloping into Teddy's room.

"Whoopee! It's party day!" Teddy yelled.

It was party day, all right, and the Taylors had a lot to celebrate!

· By four-thirty that afternoon, the grounds of Animal Inn were swarming with people of all ages and animals of all descriptions. Bright-colored balloons bobbed overhead, and crepe-paper streamers decorated the Small Animal Clinic and the new wing. Sparky's mother, Jill's mother, and Pat Dempwolf were helping Mrs. Racer pile the guests' plates high with delicious food. Toby was helping his father and his brothers scoop out ice cream for humans and animals alike. Teddy and his friends were everywhere, dodging in and out among the guests, and Erin and her best friend, Olivia, were daintily licking their ice-cream cones, trying not to drip on their pretty dresses.

"I'm glad Erin likes the hair bow I gave her," Donna Hartman said, coming up next to Val and Jill. "It looks nice with that dress she's wearing. I'm sorry she's not going to keep helping me with the grooming — she has a real talent for it. But I guess her dancing's more important. I bet she'll be a big ballet star some day."

"How about some more popcorn, Donna?" Jill said. "I made it myself."

"I've had plenty," Donna said, laughing. "Jim says if I don't stop eating like a hog, our baby's gonna be a *piglet!*" She looked down at Spotty, the Hartmans' dalmatian, who was pulling at his leash, trying to get to the dishes of kibble Val and Toby had set out. "Okay, Spotty, I'm coming."

As she hurried off, Jill said to Val, "Did you tell her about what Erin did to Marie Antoinette?"

Val shook her head. "Nope. There was no need."

"Are the Bascombes coming to the party?" Jill asked.

"I don't know, but I hope so — I like Lila's father, and Lila was nice when Dad and I brought Toni back the other night. I think maybe she's changed. Toni's accident really shook her up."

Jill raised one eyebrow. "Lila, nice? Ha! I'll believe that when I see it."

"Well, you're going to. Here she comes now."

Lila was threading her way through the crowd with Marie Antoinette at her side. Lila was wearing a bright pink dress, and the poodle's leash and rhinestone-studded collar were the exact same shade.

"Whatever you do, *don't* laugh at Toni's haircut," Val warned Jill.

Jill stifled a giggle at the sight of the little dog. But she said solemnly, "I won't."

"Hi, Lila," Val said as Lila and Toni came up to her. She bent down and patted the poodle, who leaped up and down, covering her face with doggy kisses. "Toni looks terrific."

"Toni *is* terrific." Lila looked around at the throng of people and animals. "She's probably the only dog here with a pedigree that stretches back hundreds and *hundreds* of years." She wrinkled her pert nose. "As a matter of fact, she's probably the only dog here that *has* a pedigree!" Just then Teddy, Sparky, Eric and Billy dashed past followed by Jocko and Sunshine. "Take your dogs for example. They're nothing but mongrels. When Toni's fur grows back, she's going to be a champion, just you wait and see."

Val and Jill looked at each other. "We'll wait," they said in unison.

As Lila and Marie Antoinette started off for the refreshment tables, Jill said, "If you ask me, Lila hasn't changed one single bit!"

Val sighed. "I guess you're right." Then she grinned. "And you know what? I couldn't care less!

Let's go get some of Curran's ice cream, Jill."

They started threading their way through the crowd and had almost reached the ice-cream stand when Mrs. Myers hailed Val.

"Yoo-hoo, Vallie! Come, Ling-ling. Say hello to Vallie, that's a good boy." She bustled up to Jill and Val with her little Pekingese trotting at her heels. Mrs. Myers was all dressed up in a bright flowered print, and Ling-ling had been groomed and fluffed within an inch of his life. "Such a *lovely* party!" Mrs. Myers chirped. "We're having a *wonderful* time, aren't we, Lingy?"

Ling-ling let out a sharp little bird-like bark.

"I'm glad you're both enjoying yourselves, Mrs. Myers," Val said politely. "Do you know my friend Jill Dearborne?"

"Can't say that I do. How do you do, dear? Did you bring a pet to the party?"

"No, I didn't," Jill said, smiling. "My kitten, Patches, would be scared to death of all these other cats and dogs."

"Well, Lingy's not. Lingy just *adores* parties, don't you, Lingy?" The Pekingese yapped again. "Where's your father, Vallie? And where's Donna? I want to tell them how *thrilled* I am about Animal Inn's new grooming parlor. And Lingy is, too, aren't you, Lingy?" This time the little dog didn't respond —

he was too busy licking up the remains of an ice-cream cone somebody had dropped. "Oh, there's Donna now. I must go and speak to her . . . now, Lingy, you leave that nasty, dirty old ice cream alone. Mama will get you a nice *clean* one for your very own!"

As she watched the two of them hurry off, Val shook her head. "I'll bet you anything she calls Dad tonight because Ling-ling has another tummy ache."

Jill said solemnly, "I promise I won't call your father if *I* get a tummy ache!"

Giggling, she and Val headed for the ice-cream stand again. But they had gone only a few steps when a booming voice called out, "Valentine Taylor!"

Startled, Val turned around to see Mr. Merrill right behind her. Mrs. Merrill was with them, and they were both smiling. Val was surprised — she hadn't really expected the Merrills to show up. She introduced them to Jill, who blurted out, "You're the man who was going to kill Val's horse!" Then she clapped her hand over her mouth, horrified at what she'd said. Val was horrified, too, but Mr. Merrill just kept on smiling. In a sports shirt and casual slacks, he looked very different than he had the last time Val had seen him when she had come to his office with her offer to buy The Ghost.

116

"We all make errors in judgment sometimes," Mr. Merrill said. "How's the old boy doing?"

"He's absolutely terrific, Mr. Merrill," Val said. "I ride him almost every day, and I'm saving up my money so he can have an operation to make him see better. Dad doesn't have the right equipment, but he knows a vet in Philadelphia who'll probably be able to do it."

Mr. Merrill nodded, beaming. "Glad to hear it." Mrs. Merrill nodded, too, but she didn't say anything. She hardly ever did. "Excellent idea, this boarding facility," Mr. Merrill went on. "Essex needs something like this. As a matter of fact, my wife and I are going to France in a few weeks to join Cassandra. You remember Cassandra, don't you, Valentine?"

"Oh, yes, I remember Cassandra very well," Val said sweetly.

"I've decided to bring our dogs to Animal Inn while we're gone," Mr. Merrill said. "I was going to board them with Dr. Callahan, but from what I've seen today, your father has a far superior setup. I'll be calling next week to make reservations."

"You'd better call first thing Tuesday morning," Val told him, "because we're just about all booked up for June and July."

Mr. Merrill reached out and patted her shoulder.

"I'm sure you'll be able to make room for *my* dogs," he said. "Come, dear — let's get some more of that delicious lemonade."

"*He* hasn't really changed a bit, either," Val whispered to Jill when the Merrills were out of earshot.

"Are we *ever* going to get our ice cream?" Jill moaned.

"Sure — right now. . . ." A sudden commotion near the Large Animal Clinic caught Val's eye. "Right after we find out what's going on over there!"

Jill rushed after her as she dodged through the crowd. When they were finally able to see what was happening, they both stopped short and began whooping with laughter. Marie Antoinette was barking wildly at Princess Tuptim, Mrs. Wentworth's prize Siamese. Tuptim, back arched, tail bristled, and blue eyes blazing, was teetering on top of the white rail fence, hissing and spitting at Marie Antoinette. And Lila was sitting in the big water trough Mike and Toby had set out for the animal guests, spitting and hissing, too. Her bright pink dress was soaking wet, and so was the rest of her. Mrs. Wentworth, hands on hips, was glaring down at her.

"Lila Bascombe, this is the limit! Call off your horried little dog *this minute*!"

"But it wasn't my fault," Lila wailed. "Toni just took off after her, and I tried to stop her, but then I tripped and fell. . . ."

"Oh, wow!" Val gasped between bursts of giggles. "The perfect end to a perfect day!"

"Better believe it!" Jill cried. Trying very hard to look properly concerned, she said. "I suppose we ought to help her out of that trough."

Val nodded. "I suppose we should." Then she grinned from ear to ear. "But let's not! Race you to the ice-cream stand!"

Animals you'll love...
a series you won't want to miss!

ANIMAL INN
by Virginia Vail

Thirteen-year-old Val Taylor looks forward to afternoons everyday! That's when she gets to spend time with a menagerie of horses, dogs, cats, and other animals, great and small. They're all residents at her dad's veterinary clinic, Animal Inn.

Look for these Apple® titles!

❑	MY43434-9	#1	**Pets Are for Keeps**	$2.75
❑	MY42787-3	#2	**A Kid's Best Friend**	$2.75
❑	MY43433-0	#3	**Monkey Business**	$2.75
❑	MY43432-2	#4	**Scaredy Cat**	$2.75
❑	MY43431-4	#5	**Adopt-a-Pet**	$2.75
❑	MY43430-6	#6	**All the Way Home**	$2.75
❑	MY42798-9	#7	**The Pet Makeover**	$2.75
❑	MY42799-7	#8	**Petnapped** (May '90)	$2.75

Available wherever you buy books...
or use the coupon below.

Scholastic Inc. P.O. Box 7502, 2932 E. McCarty Street, Jefferson City, MO 65102

Please send me the books I have checked above. I am enclosing $ _____
(please add $2.00 to cover shipping and handling). Send check or money order—no cash or C.O.D.'s please.

Name _____

Address _____

City _____ State/Zip _____

Please allow four to six weeks for delivery. Offer good in U.S.A. only.
Sorry, mail order not available to residents of Canada. Prices subject to change.

AI889